"I suppose we should ge[...] get a good night's sleep[...]"

Without warning, Sebas[...] edge of the gate, causing her dress's hem [...] up her thighs. And while she made the appropriate adjustments, he climbed into the truck bed and had the nerve to position himself behind her, his long legs dangling on either side of hers. "Are you comfortable?" he asked as he circled his arms around her middle.

"No, I am not. I cannot have a decent conversation when I cannot see your face."

"You only have to listen to my voice."

Oh, that voice. That low, grainy bedroom voice that had enticed her on so many nights. And days. No matter how deep their conflicts had run, he had always been able to seduce her into submission.

Nasira found herself leaning back against him, and turning her thoughts to the danger in succumbing to his power. "This is wrong, Sebastian," she said with little conviction.

"This is right, sweetheart. You're my wife."

* * *

In Pursuit of His Wife is part of the Texas Cattleman's Club: Lies and Lullabies series—Baby secrets and a scheming sheikh rock Royal, Texas

Dear Reader,

It's been a while since I've visited Royal, but I'm sure glad to be back. A lot of things have changed with the legendary Texas Cattleman's Club, yet some aspects remain the same—dashing heroes and strong heroines populate the town in their quest for love.

I do have to admit that I've wondered about past characters I've had the pleasure to write, including one of my favorite TCC members, Darin Shakir, from *Fit for a Sheikh*. For that reason I grabbed the opportunity to reconnect with the mysterious military tracker and his feisty lover, Fiona. I'll only say they've been mighty busy during the past decade, and they've proven to be the perfect example of a happily married couple.

Nasira and Sebastian Edwards, whose convenient marriage is in crisis, need all the help they can get. Their journey won't be easy, but Royal is a magical place where miracles occur when least expected. I'd bet the ranch that this husband and wife just might be lucky enough to claim one of their own.

Happy reading and happy trails!

Kristi

KRISTI GOLD

IN PURSUIT OF HIS WIFE

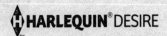

Special thanks and acknowledgment are
given to Kristi Gold for her contribution
to the Texas Cattleman's Club: Lies and
Lullabies miniseries.

Recycling programs
for this product may
not exist in your area

ISBN-13: 978-0-373-73457-3

In Pursuit of His Wife

Copyright © 2016 by Harlequin Books S.A.

HARLEQUIN®

™ www.Harlequin.com

Printed in U.S.A.

Kristi Gold has a fondness for beaches, baseball and bridal reality shows. She firmly believes that love has remarkable healing powers, and she feels very fortunate to be able to weave stories of love and commitment. As a bestselling author, a National Readers' Choice Award winner and a three-time Romance Writers of America RITA® Award finalist, Kristi has learned that although accolades are wonderful, the most cherished rewards come from networking with readers. She can be reached through her website at kristigold.com, or through Facebook.

Books by Kristi Gold

HARLEQUIN DESIRE

The Return of the Sheikh
One Night with the Sheikh
From Single Mom to Secret Heiress
The Sheikh's Son
One Hot Desert Night
The Sheikh's Secret Heir

Texas Extreme

The Rancher's Marriage Pact

Texas Cattleman's Club: Lies and Lullabies

In Pursuit of His Wife

Visit her Author Profile page at Harlequin.com, or kristigold.com, for more titles.

One

Seated in a wicker glider on the mansion's stately porch, Nasira Edwards admired the beauty of the Wild Aces, the ranch her brother, Rafiq, had bought his beloved bride-to-be, Violet. Nasira appreciated the way landscaped lawns gave way to green pastureland. She relished the warm May breeze, the climate so different from London this time of year. When she had originally traveled to Royal, Texas—home to the legendary Texas Cattleman's Club—she had done so to prevent Rafe from exacting revenge on his friend, Mac, for a mistake she had made over a decade ago. She had come to clear the air, right past wrongs, and fortunately she had succeeded. Yet that had not been the only reason behind the journey. She yearned for the peace this place could provide, yet peace had not come. The lingering pain of loss was simply too overwhelming.

In response to the memories, she withdrew the bracelet from the pocket of her dress and studied the tiny silver rattle charm she had received upon confirming her pregnancy. A surprising gift from a husband who had not embraced fatherhood. Still, she had viewed the welcome gesture as a symbol of hope for a bright future, until the day all hope had been splintered like shards of fragile glass.

Her palm automatically came to rest on her abdomen, now as barren as her life had been for a while. The baby she had so desperately wanted, and tragically miscarried, had changed her completely. Odd how she could miss someone she had known for such a brief time. And strange how badly she missed Sebastian, though he had been emotionally absent for the past six months. She had had no choice but to continue to put physical distance between them in an effort to reassess their future.

When the door opened to her left, Nasira expected to find her brother, Rafiq, checking on her welfare. Instead, Rafe's friend, Mac McCallum, stepped outside and gave her a pleasant smile. "Are you doing okay?"

She did not deserve his good humor or respect after what she had done to him in the distant past. "I've been enjoying the Texas sunset."

"Looks to me like that old sun has been gone a while," he said. "My sister sent me out here to tell you dinner will be ready in a few."

Food held little appeal in recent days. "I appreciate Violet's hospitality, but I am not very hungry."

"Suit yourself, but if you keep going this way, you'll be blown to New Mexico if the wind picks up steam."

She smiled reluctantly and stood. "I suppose if that is a possibility, I should attempt to eat something. Are you staying for dinner?"

"Not tonight. I'm meeting up with Andrea."

Nasira suspected Mac had feelings for his personal assistant that went beyond the boardroom, even if he could not admit it to himself, according to her future sister-in-law, Violet. "Is this business or pleasure?"

He frowned. "Business, of course."

"It's rather late in the day for that, is it not?"

"Unfortunately it comes with the territory of Mc-Callum Enterprises."

When the discussion lulled, Nasira saw her chance to verbally make amends for past mistakes. She studied the wooden planks beneath her feet for a moment before regarding him again. "I wanted to extend another apology for what I did to you all those years ago. The guilt has been unbearable."

Mac lifted his shoulders in a shrug. "Hey, you were young. We were both young. You were just trying to get out of an arranged marriage to a man twice your age."

That ill-fated visit to the university to stay with her brother had set a horrible course that had led to Rafe's need for revenge. "Yet I was wrong to use you to achieve that goal, especially when I climbed into your bed for the sole purpose of having my father discover us. And because our father blamed Rafe for not looking after me, that led to his determination to seek revenge on you. I shudder to think what might have happened had I not come here to intervene."

"It all turned out okay," Mac said. "He's no longer trying to buy up the town to get back at me, he's going to marry my sister, and we're going to be one big happy family."

Nasira was happy for them all, but still… "Even after Rafe's torture and confinement for years due to my errors in judgment, he has forgiven me. I suppose I need to know if you will forgive me as well, though I would understand if you would not."

"Consider it done, Nasira. That's old water under the bridge now that Rafe knows I didn't really sleep with you. And since he's marrying my sister, I consider us all one big happy family."

Relief washed over her, though she couldn't claim to be happy over the state of her own marriage. "I so appreciate your understanding."

"No problem. Mind if I ask you something?"

"Not at all."

He raked a hand through his dark blond hair. "Don't take this wrong, but I'm wondering what the hell your husband was thinking when he let you get away?"

The course of the conversation made her somewhat uncomfortable. "It is rather complicated. Sebastian is complicated. After ten years of marriage, at times I wonder if I know him at all."

"One thing I do know. When a man doesn't realize the value of his wife, that's borrowing trouble. I just hope he comes around soon and realizes what he'd be giving up."

If only she could believe Sebastian had the capacity to be transformed into someone who would fight for their relationship. "I truly appreciate your concern and understanding, Mac."

"You're welcome. Guess I'll be heading home to the Double M now." He started toward the steps but paused and faced her again. "Before I leave, I'd just like to say it's fairly clear you don't need another big brother, but if you ever want a sounding board, you know where to find me."

How nice to come upon such a benevolent man. She certainly had not received so much compassion from her own husband in quite some time. "Thank you."

Mac returned to her and rested his palms on her shoulders. "Keep your chin up and keep standing your ground. You deserve the best."

Until six months ago, she had believed she had been blessed with the best of everything. Almost. "For the sake of clarification, Sebastian is not mean or cruel. He is simply too controlled and at times, distant. I have often wished he would lower his guard and demonstrate some sort of emotion, but I've accepted that it will most likely never happen—"

"Unhand my wife, you bloody bastard!"

Nasira barely had time to comprehend what she had heard before her estranged husband rushed onto the porch, drew back his fist and hit Mac in the chin, knocking the rancher backward against the brick wall.

When Mac gave Sebastian a menacing look, Nasira returned to reality in time to step between the men. "What are you doing, Sebastian?"

He pointed at Mac and sent him a menacing glare. "I'll not allow another man to grope my wife."

Never had she'd seen Sebastian act this way, and as much as she deplored violence, and despite her shock over his sudden appearance, she was pleasantly surprised, albeit somewhat mortified. "Oh, for goodness' sake. He is only a friend and he was not groping me."

Mac pushed away from the wall, rubbed his chin and glared at Sebastian. "If I didn't think so highly of your wife and her brother, I'd invite you to take this out into the yard and finish it, you jackass."

Sebastian balled his fists at his sides. "I would be glad to finish this."

Nasira spun on her husband. "Stop this right now, Sebastian. No one will be fighting if I have any say in the matter, and I do." She turned back to her friend and sent him an apologetic look. "Mac, I am so very sorry for my husband's behavior. I assure you he's not normally so impulsive with total strangers. And if you would not mind, I would like a few moments alone with him."

"No problem," Mac said before turning an acrid look on Sebastian. "I'm going to give you a pass, Edwards, and only because you're Nasira's husband. But don't push your luck by trying something like that again."

Sebastian straightened his tie and smirked. "If I find you touching Nasira again, I cannot promise there won't be a repeat performance."

"Just take better care of your wife and you won't have to worry about me."

After Mac disappeared into the darkness, Nasira prepared for a confrontation. "What were you thinking, and why on earth are you here?"

Sebastian opened and closed his fist. "I wasn't thinking, only reacting to a man with his hands on my wife. A man from her past, no less. And I have come to escort that wife back to London."

Her fury began to escalate. "First of all, nothing ever existed between myself and Mac, other than he was attempting to assist me in fooling my father into believing I'd been compromised."

"He looked as if he would like to compromise you in earnest a few moments ago."

She refused to give credence to his suspicions. "Your imagination is evidently running wild. And most important, I am not your property, Sebastian. I will return when I decide to return. *If* I decide to return."

"You're my wife. You belong with me."

At least he hadn't said she belonged *to* him, as if that were any consolation. "I came here to gain some perspective and I am going to stay until that is accomplished. You might as well climb back on the jet and wait at home for word from me."

"I refuse to go until this issue is resolved."

Despite his stubborn attitude, Nasira began to notice how handsome he looked and knew immediately she would lose her determination if he stayed. Too much time had passed since they had made love—the one thing that had always been right with their convenient marriage. Yet that had been his decision, not hers. "At the very least I will be here until Rafe and Violet's wedding at the end of the month."

"I'll wait as long as it takes."

She brought out the best argument to convince him to go—the shipping business he owned and ran. "I cannot believe you would ignore your duties and abandon the company for any length of time."

"I own the company. I can do what I please."

Such a frustrating man. "Do you have an answer for everything?"

He sent her a slow, easy smile. The smile he had given her all those years ago from across a very crowded ballroom, as if they had been thrust into a storybook scene. The smile that had convinced her to enter into an arrangement to escape her father's clutches. "Have you had dinner?"

No, and she had begun to feel the effects. "I have not, although Violet has prepared a meal."

"I'm certain she will understand if you would rather dine with your husband. We could continue our discussion then."

While Nasira took a moment to consider her options, the door swung open again and out walked Rafe, her tall, dark, handsome overly-protective brother.

He immediately eyed Sebastian with disapproval. "I see you did not follow my advice and remain in London, brother-in-law."

Sebastian looked equally miffed. "And when we spoke by phone two days ago, I made it quite clear I would make that decision without your interference."

Nasira stared at her husband before returning her attention to her sibling. "Rafiq bin Saleed, why did you not tell me you spoke with Sebastian?"

Rafe did not appear the least bit contrite. "You mentioned on numerous occasions you did not want to be disturbed by him."

"And he refused to allow me to speak with you when you ignored my calls to your cell," Sebastian added.

She despised it when men insisted she could not look after herself. "You had no right to take the choice out of my hands, Rafe."

"It makes little difference now," Sebastian said. "I'm here and I intend to make the best of the situation."

She only wished she knew what else he intended. That information would only be gained if she accepted his invitation to dine with him tonight. "I'm going to accompany Sebastian to dinner. I will be gone an hour or so."

"Do you believe that is wise, Nasira?" Rafe asked.

"We bloody believe that is none—"

"I can speak for myself, Sebastian. I am no longer your charge, Rafe. I can take care of myself. Tell Violet I truly appreciate her hospitality. We should go now, Sebastian, before I change my mind."

With that, Nasira followed Sebastian down the porch steps and when she didn't immediately spot a sedan, she paused on the pavement. "How did you arrive here?"

He nodded toward a shiny black truck at the end of the drive. "This is all they had available to rent at the airport."

Nasira covered her mouth to keep from laughing. "Oh, my. Can you handle that?"

He looked somewhat incensed over what he apparently considered an insult to his masculinity. "Of course I can handle it. I made it here, did I not?"

"All right," she said, and then continued toward the monstrosity.

Once there, Sebastian opened the passenger door and held out his hand. "Your cowboy chariot, madam. Let me assist you."

"I am almost six feet tall, Sebastian. I can manage climbing into a truck by myself."

"Only trying to be a gentleman, Sira."

The sound of his pet name for her stopped Nasira in her tracks. "Do you know how long it has been since you called me that?"

He winked. "Perhaps too long."

She had no clue where all the charm and machismo had been hiding. Following the miscarriage, he had spent long hours at work and little time with her. Perhaps he had turned a corner that would lead to change. Only time would tell. In the interim, Nasira would remain cautiously optimistic.

As they sat in the red booth in the Royal Diner, Sebastian found his wife to be predictably cool. And as always, very beautiful. The white cotton dress fit her to perfection, contrasting with her long, dark hair draped over her slender shoulders. Since her departure, he'd spent many a night in their bed, longing for her company. Since the loss of their child, he'd spent most of his time avoiding her out of fear. Not fear of her. Fear of losing her. Yet that was exactly what he had done by pushing her away. A bloody self-fulfilling prophecy that he couldn't explain without baring raw emotions.

Pushing the thoughts away, he turned his attention to the plastic-covered menu and scanned the unpalatable selections. "What do you recommend, Sira? The double cheeseburger or the fried catfish plate?"

That earned him her smile. "I realize this place isn't exactly your cup of tea, but I find it charming."

"I find it overly quaint and a heart attack waiting to happen."

"They do have salads and I hear the grilled chicken is very good."

He closed the menu and set it aside. "I will make do with the limited choices."

"What are you having?"

A tremendous urge to kiss her. "I'm going to sample the steak. And you?"

She laid the red-checkered napkin in her lap. "Definitely a salad."

"You should eat something a bit heartier. You're too thin."

"I am the same weight as I was before I left London."

"I'm only concerned about you, Sira."

She sent him a skeptical look. "Oh really? Where was all this concern over the past six months?"

He didn't feel this was the time or the place to get into such a serious subject, and thankfully a waitress arrived to interrupt their conversation.

She patted her rather large blond hair, pulled a pencil from behind her ear and a notepad from the pocket of the red apron. "Howdy. I'm Darla. What can I get the two of you darlin's to drink? Maybe some sweet tea?"

He couldn't quite fathom these strange Texas customs. "I prefer to sweeten my tea myself. With sugar and milk."

"She means cold tea," Nasira said. "I will take a glass with lemon."

He needed something much stronger to make it through this evening. "Bring me ale."

The woman raised a painted eyebrow. "Ginger ale?"

Bloody hell. "Beer."

"Sebastian, I cannot drive that truck," Nasira said. "For that reason, I suggest you forego the ale."

She did have a point and in accordance with his plan, he needed to prove himself worthy of her company. "Water will be fine."

"With lemon?" Darla asked.

"Why not? If that is fine with my wife."

Nasira frowned. "Of course it is. And I would like a salad with the dressing on the side."

"She would also like the grilled chicken," Sebastian added despite Nasira's disapproving look. "I'll have the rib eye. Make certain it's cooked through."

Darla looked somewhat appalled. "You mean well done?"

"Precisely."

The waitress jotted down the order then gathered the menus. "You two aren't from around here, are you?"

Sebastian sent her a mock grin. "What gave us away?"

"The men around here order their meat rare." With that, Darla waddled away, muttering under her breath.

Nasira immediately turned a sharp gaze on him. "Why do you insist on doing that?"

He opted to play ignorant. "Doing what?"

"Ordering my meals for me. I am quite capable of deciding what and how much I eat."

"I've always ordered for you, Sira."

"I know and I do not care for it."

"And you waited ten years to tell me?"

"It seemed simpler not to make waves and avoid conflict."

Did she think so little of him? "I'm not your father, Nasira. If you want something from me, you need only ask."

She stared at him a few moments. "I want another baby."

The one thing he felt he could not give her. "Impossible."

"Why, Sebastian?"

He could only offer her a partial truth. "You had a devil of a time when you miscarried. The doctor said—"

"That I am quite capable of conceiving again and carrying to full term. The risk is not any greater than any woman who has lost a child in the first trimester."

He imagined his own mother had believed that very thing. "Look, this is not the time or the place to discuss this."

She lifted her chin and leveled a determined glare on him. "Unless we discuss it, I will not be returning to London with you in the foreseeable future."

Sebastian swallowed around his shock. Not once during their time together had she issued threats. "We will talk about this some other time."

The waitress returned with their drinks, and they waited in silence for their order to arrive. All conversation ceased as they ate food that was surprisingly palatable. He spent a good deal of time watching the patrons, when he wasn't watching his wife pick at her meal.

Unfortunately, she only afforded him a glance when he asked, "How do you find the fare?"

"Adequate," she said and then took another bite.

He wondered if he would spend the next few days dealing with one-word answers while attempting to convince her to come home. Would she rebuff his advances, or eventually return to what they once had? He longed for the latter. He longed for her. All of her. First, he had to regain her trust and respect, if at this juncture, and in light of his mistakes, that were even possible.

By the time he had paid the bill, Sebastian worried he had ruined his chances at reconciliation.

Not yet. Not until he convinced her they belonged together, with or without children. How exactly he would achieve that goal remained to be seen. He knew only one way to do this—by using a tried and true technique that had never failed to turn her into clay in his hands.

"Sebastian, what are you doing?"

"Finding a private place to talk."

He had definitely found it, Nasira realized when he continued past the Wild Aces and took a dirt road that forked to the right. Once he reached the fence line, he backed the truck up beneath some low-hanging tree branches.

Before Nasira could voice a protest, Sebastian slid out of the seat, rounded the hood and opened her door. "Now if you will come with me please."

Clearly he had taken leave of his senses. "I refuse to traipse around in the dark, Sebastian."

"We're not going to traipse. We're going to sit in the back of this truck."

She felt certain that might not be in her best interests. "Why can we not remain in the front seat?"

"Because it's a beautiful night that should be spent beneath the stars and the moon."

She started to say they could barely see the stars but the opportunity to respond was lost when he reached in, took her by the waist, and lifted her out and onto her feet. "First that dreadful fight with Mac, and now you are manhandling me like some Neanderthal. What has come over you?"

"My behavior isn't necessarily so out-of-character for me, though it's been quite a few years since I've engaged in it."

Nasira released a cynical laugh. "You will have a difficult time convincing me that you ever behaved in that manner. In all the years I've known you, I have never seen you raise your voice, much less your hand."

He smiled. "Oh, you would be surprised what a scrapper I was in my formative years. I managed to get tossed out of three boarding schools before I finally settled down in my final year before university."

She could barely make out his smile, but she could

hear the pride in his voice. "That is definitely news to me and frankly somewhat appalling."

He leaned over and brushed a kiss across her cheek. "Are you certain you're appalled, or did it perhaps impress you?"

It had both surprised and in some ways set her senses on fire, not that she would dare make that admission. "It served to remind me what ridiculously volatile creatures men can be."

"Let's find a place to sit before we continue this conversation."

As long as they remained upright, she should be safe from giving in to his sensual charms. Then again, he had not attempted to touch her in so long, she could not even imagine that would be his goal. "Fine. But I only wish to stay for a while. I am fatigued from all the drama tonight."

"No more drama," he said as he took her by the hand and led her to the rear of the vehicle. "Now to ascertain how this bloody thing opens."

Before Sebastian could make a move to investigate, Nasira pulled the latch and lowered the tailgate. "It is really quite simple."

"How did you learn to do that?" he asked, sheer awe in his tone.

She shrugged. "I've seen Rafiq open one."

Sebastian reached out and brushed her hair away from her shoulder. "You are truly an amazing woman."

"Why? Because I can trip a release on a truck?"

"Because you are so observant and incredibly beautiful."

As much as she appreciated the compliment, she also recognized he had never paid her many, except about her physical attributes. "Thank you. I suppose we should get this over with so I can get a good night's sleep."

Without warning, he hoisted her up on the edge of the gate, causing her dress's hem to ride up her thighs. And while she made the appropriate adjustments, he climbed into the truck bed and had the nerve to position himself behind her, his long legs dangling on either side of hers. "Are you comfortable?" he asked as he circled his arms around her middle.

Uncomfortable would be more accurate; she didn't—or shouldn't—welcome the close contact. "No, I am not. I cannot have a decent conversation when I cannot see your face."

"You only have to listen to my voice."

Oh, that voice. That low, grainy bedroom voice that had enticed her on so many nights. And days. No matter how deep their conflicts had run, he had always been able to seduce her into submission. Granted, she had done her share of seducing as well, including the night she had conceived their child—without telling him she had stopped taking her birth control pills, which was information she had concealed until she had confirmed the pregnancy. Somehow he had forgiven the deception, or so he had said, yet she believed he had never forgotten it.

Nasira found herself leaning back against him, and turning her thoughts to the danger of succumbing to his power when he moved her hair aside and feathered kisses on her neck. "This is wrong, Sebastian," she said with little conviction.

"Remember that night in the carriage?" he said, proving he was bent on ignoring her concerns.

"Yes, I remember." How could she forget? On their honeymoon, he had arranged for a horse-drawn tour of Bath, which had led to taboo touching beneath the blanket, all leading up to a night she would never forget. The night she had lost her virginity and in some ways, her heart.

He slid one palm down her throat and traveled beneath the bodice where he cupped her breast through the lace bra. "I recall you were trembling, as you are now."

She hadn't noticed that at all. Her attention remained drawn to his fingertip circling her nipple now bound in a tight knot. "I was somewhat nervous."

"You were hot," he whispered. "I imagine you're hot now."

Before Nasira could prepare, Sebastian parted her legs with his free hand while sliding his other underneath the bra. "Pull your dress up to your waist."

The request was both startling and highly erotic. "Why?"

"So you might see what I'm doing to you."

As badly as she wanted his attention, she did not wish to make another grave mistake by giving in too soon. "This behavior will solve nothing, Sebastian."

He continued to fondle her breast without missing a beat. "I disagree. It will solve our need for each other. It will serve to remind us how we've always needed each other."

several, including your lack of trust in me and your resistance to having another child."

He slid out of the truck to tuck in his shirt. "We have a month to work out our differences and reach a compromise."

If they could work anything out. Nasira was not certain they could. "Presently I need to return to the house and you need to return to wherever you are staying for the duration."

He streaked a palm over his nape. "Actually, I haven't a place to stay at this point in time. It appears there are no rooms in the inns due to some rodeo event in the area."

Of all the irresponsible, ridiculous excuses. "You did not make arrangements before you decided to travel here?"

"It was a spontaneous plan."

An illogical plan in her opinion. "I can't very well have you in my room under my brother's roof. He is well aware we're having problems, and I prefer we not sleep in the same bed until we've had more time to work on our issues."

"I will take whatever room they have available if you don't wish me in your bed."

"There isn't another room, Sebastian. The house is still undergoing renovations and I have the only accommodations left."

"Then I suppose I shall sleep in the truck until other arrangements can be made."

Oh, for heaven's sake. "All right. You may stay in my room as long as you have no expectations and you

So caught up in his seduction, she clung to the last thread of sanity, relying on bitter memories to maintain her composure. "You haven't been concerned about my needs for months."

He kissed her cheek. "I know, and I'm bent on making up for my neglect. Can we for once stop thinking and allow ourselves only pleasure for a while?"

"But—"

He brought her head around and kissed her soundly. "Let me make love to you, Sira. Please."

She should issue a protest, she should be more resistant, yet she had become too caught up in the anticipation of how she knew he could—and would—make her feel. Too sexually charged over witnessing a side of him she had never seen before this evening—the jealous side, willing to defend her honor.

After she complied, he whispered, "Take off your panties."

This time she didn't hesitate to follow his directive, and after she lifted her hips and slid the lace down to her thighs, she no longer questioned the wisdom in allowing this to happen. After all, he was not a stranger. He was her husband, and she had been without intimacy for much too long.

While Nasira watched, Sebastian moved to the apex of her thighs and began to stroke her. A flood of heat and dampness caused her breath to catch in her chest. He knew how much pressure to apply. How to tease her into oblivion. The moments seemed so surreal—both of them in the back of a truck out in the wide open spaces of Texas, a warm breeze blowing across her face, her husband's hand between her legs bringing her closer and closer to the threshold of orgasm. She wanted badly to keep it at bay, to keep her eyes open, but all to no avail. When Sebastian slid a finger inside her, whispered a few words some might find crude, the climax crashed into her, bringing with it a series of strong spasms.

Nasira was barely aware that Sebastian had taken his hand away, but very aware when he moved beside her. When she heard the rasp of a zipper, she opened her eyes to see that he had shoved his slacks down his hips, revealing what the spontaneous foreplay had physically done to him.

"I need you, sweetheart," he whispered. "Come here."

She needed him as well. Much more than she should. "You want us to lie down in the back of this truck? I question the comfort in that." She also questioned her own sanity.

He grinned. "Who said anything about lying down? I am relinquishing control to you and hoping for a memorable ride."

Awareness over what he had intimated sent Nasira's pulse on a sprint. Every word he uttered seemed to be a jolt to her libido. Every suggestion added fuel to the building fire. Realizing the fit of the dress might not allow for enough room, she hopped to her feet to face her husband. She boldly unzipped the dress, pulled it over her head, tossed it and the bra into the bed of the truck and then pushed the panties down where they fell to the ground. She was totally, unabashedly naked and remarkably ready to finish this interlude immediately.

With that in mind, she climbed back into the truck on her knees to straddle Sebastian's thighs. Yet he thwarted that immediate plan when he said, "Wait."

She didn't want to delay another moment. "Why?"

"Birth control," he grated out.

Of course that would be his primary focus, and it should be hers as well. She lowered from her knees and sat on the gate, hugging her arms to her breasts. "I have not resumed taking the pills. I had no reason to do that."

She saw dismay in his expression before he stood and pulled up his slacks. "And you should have informe me immediately."

She suddenly felt very exposed, both physically emotionally. She also sensed a hint of accusation i tone. "If you are intimating I planned this so you impregnate me, I was not the one who drove h the purposes of seduction."

He released a rough sigh. "You're right, and ogies for doubting your motives. However, if sider our past, you certainly shouldn't blan my concerns."

Furious, Nasira came to her feet and g discarded clothing. "Obviously allowing th under the circumstances has been a colos

She glimpsed anger in his expressio pulled the dress over her head, heard when he said, "The sounds you made you certainly enjoyed it."

"Evidently I am not immune to y said. "But mark my words, this will until we come to terms with our iss

leave before first light. I truly do not wish to explain your presence to Rafiq or to have him assume we've been…you know."

"I'm certain Rafe has engaged in…you know, since his intended is living with him."

"She is also pregnant," she added, curious to see how he might react.

"Really?" he said with little enthusiasm. "I didn't know the old boy had it in him."

"He does, and he is very protective of Violet, as well as me. On the other hand, he is not particularly fond of you at the moment. He assumes you have done something to wound me."

"And clearly you have allowed him to have those assumptions."

"Like it or not, Sebastian, your behavior for the past few months has been very hurtful to me."

He sighed. "And that is why I'm here now, to atone for my transgressions. Regardless, I promise to remain on my side of the bed until you are ready for me to fully atone."

When he suggestively winked, Nasira realized having Sebastian in her bed would not be wise for many reasons. "I will make a place for you on the floor."

He had the nerve to kiss her hand. "Whatever you wish, fair lady."

She wanted not to be so attracted him. She wanted not to want him, yet sadly she still did. "It is late," she said as she wrenched from his grasp. "And one more thing. When we arrive, be quiet. I prefer not to wake the household."

Two

"What is he doing here?"

Sebastian had barely entered the two-story foyer before being verbally accosted by his brother-in-law. "I'm accompanying my wife to the bedroom."

With her hand on the banister, Nasira sent a sheepish glance in Rafe's direction. "He does not have a hotel room for the night. However, he has promised to leave first thing tomorrow morning."

Rafe gestured toward a formal floral settee. "The sofa is available."

Angry over the suggestion, Sebastian dropped his bags on the ground. "I won't fit on the bloody sofa. And if you recall, I'm still married to your sister and I have every right to sleep with her. Once you're married, you'll soon learn that problems can and will arise in every union."

Rafiq took a step toward the stairs. "She does not want you here."

"I invited him, Rafe," Nasira said. "But only for the night. Now if you will excuse us, we are both exhausted from the evening's events."

"Quite memorable events," Sebastian added knowing he would probably incur his wife's wrath.

Rafe pointed at him. "I do not wish to see you here when I awaken."

Sebastian saluted. "Yes, sir, commander sheikh."

Without looking back, Nasira hurried up the stairs and paused at the landing before regarding Sebastian again. "Are you coming?"

He suddenly realized he should attempt to turn Rafe into an ally, not an enemy. "In a moment. I'd like to have a word with your brother."

He saw a fleeting look of panic in her eyes. "All right, if you two promise to remain civil."

A promise Sebastian hoped he could keep. "I have no problem with that."

She glanced past him toward her brother. "Rafiq?"

"I will maintain my calm," Rafe said.

"I am counting on that," Nasira said before she climbed the remaining stairs and disappeared.

Sebastian decided he could use a bit of a pick-me-up and with that in mind, he grabbed up the smaller bag, set it on the sofa, unzipped it and withdrew a bottle of mediocre scotch, the only thing he had been able to find at the lone liquor store in town. "Would you care to join me in a drink?"

"No, I would not," Rafe said.

"Then would you mind providing a glass. I find it somewhat uncouth to drink from the bottle."

Without speaking, Rafe left through a door at the back of the parlor. He returned a few moments later with a crystal tumbler he set on the white coffee table before taking a seat in a club chair across from the sofa. Sebastian poured himself a glass of the amber liquid. Though he preferred ice, he thought it best not to press his luck.

After taking a long drink, Sebastian settled in on the settee as the low-quality scotch burned down his throat. At this rate, the combination of booze and jet lag could very well land him on his arse. Of course, he could rest assured he would sleep well…on the bedroom floor.

"Where is your lovely fiancée?" he began when Rafe failed to speak.

"She is sleeping," he replied. "The pregnancy has fatigued her greatly."

Sebastian remembered that all too well from the time when Sira was carrying their child. He also remembered the sound of her mournful cries when she had lost that child. "I'm sure the wedding plans have also contributed to that fatigue. How are you faring with that, by the way?"

Rafe crossed one leg over the other. "I have left the preparation up to the women. I only require knowing where I need to be and when I should be there."

Sebastian doubted he would escape that easily. "I suppose that is probably best."

Rafe inclined his head and studied him. "I suspect you did not detain me so you could speak about wedding plans."

Sebastian finished off the scotch with a grimace and poured another glass. "No. I felt it necessary to outline my intentions toward your sister. Has she mentioned me at all?"

"She only intimated your marriage is in shambles and hinted the breakdown is due to your inattentiveness."

As hard as it was to hear, he couldn't debate that assessment. "I've only had her welfare in mind since the miscarriage. I wanted to give her as much space as she needed. I realize now that was probably a bloody bad idea to show up, unannounced."

"Yes, and it has created a problem that will not be easy to rectify."

It occurred to Sebastian that he could possibly elevate Rafe's opinion of him if he appealed to his ego by asking for advice. "You seem to be a man who knows the workings of a woman's mind. Do you have a suggestion on how I could get back in Nasira's good graces?"

Rafe didn't seem to be flattered, though. "Perhaps you should return to London and allow her to decide if she wants to resume the marriage."

Not the answer he'd hoped for. "Look, Rafe, we've invested ten years in this union—"

"Convenient union, not a love match," Rafe added.

Point reluctantly taken. "Nevertheless, I care greatly for your sister and I'm not willing to give up what we've had for a decade without a fight. But I need assistance in order to win her back. Who better to help me than her brother, who knows her better than most?"

When Rafe remained silent, Sebastian almost gave up until his brother-in-law said, "Shower her with small tokens of your affection."

"You mean flowers and jewelry?"

Rafe looked at him as if he were a total dimwit. "Not only material gifts. And do not concentrate solely on sexual matters."

No sex or hearts and flowers. What was left? "I'm afraid I am still at a loss."

"I have learned women appreciate gestures that might seem insignificant to most men," Rafe said. "They greatly enjoy breakfast in bed. Massages. Having their hair washed."

Sebastian could handle any and all of those things, as long as he had some privacy to do them. "I now understand what you're saying, but I do have another problem. If I am going to woo her, I bloody can't do it in a hotel."

"And I do not wish to witness this wooing." Rafe came to his feet. "I have a possible solution to your lodging issues."

Sebastian finished his second drink and stood, realizing all too well that he should have stopped with the first scotch. He'd always been able to hold his liquor but at the moment he felt as if he could fly without the benefit of his corporate jet. "What do you have in mind?"

"A private residence where you could reside during the duration of your stay. The owners are friends of a friend and they will be leaving for a trip out of the country for two months. I will call tomorrow and let you know if they are amenable to the request. It will be up to you to convince Nasira, without coercion, to join you."

Sebastian had no intention of coercing her. Not when he had other ways to convince her. "I'll try to persuade her."

"If you are unsuccessful, will you agree to return to London?"

Only if and when he had exhausted every option. "That seems fair enough."

"Good. I am going to retire now. I will inform you in the morning if I have secured the accommodations."

"Thank you, Rafe. I certainly value your opinions and your willingness to assist me."

The man seemed unimpressed with Sebastian's gratitude. "I am doing this for Nasira. Her happiness is paramount. I will not tolerate anyone who does not respect her wishes. Keep that in mind as you move forward with your goal."

Before Sebastian could respond, Rafe turned and started up the stairs without looking back. Sebastian dropped down on the settee and rubbed both hands over his face. If he didn't get up soon, he could end up sleeping on the sardine-can sofa.

On that thought, he trudged up the stairs and made his way to his reluctant bride's boudoir. He rapped on the door and when he didn't get a response, entered the room to the sounds of running water.

He had one of two options—leave and let her have her privacy, or shower her with affection in the shower. Option two earned his vote. As long as he proceeded with caution.

He stripped off his shirt, inadvertently popping a button, then sat on the edge of the mattress to toe out of his shoes. He carelessly kicked them off, barely missing the French doors leading to a balcony. In an effort to compose himself, he removed his slacks and underwear with more patience, then tossed them aside on the window seat to his right. When he rose from the bed, he realized he would have to keep a tight hold on his libido. He also realized he wasn't the only one standing.

"Down, old chap," he muttered when he walked to the door, then paused to take a deep breath to regain some semblance of control.

If he played his cards correctly, this could be the first step in demonstrating that he could be the kind husband his wife needed.

Nasira needed a shower and a good night's sleep. She also needed to know exactly what Sebastian was saying to her brother, but that could wait until morning.

Standing beneath the spray, she closed her eyes, bent on washing away the memories of those intimate moments under the stars in the rear—of all things— a Texas truck. Still, her mind whirled back to the interlude and the way Sebastian had so easily unearthed sensations she had greatly missed. Sensations she still experienced with a succession of tremors and tingling. Her husband had so masterfully manipulated her into oblivion with only a few strokes, and once more the heat began to make itself known....

Nasira shook off the images, stepped to the side of the spray and opened her eyes, determined to regain some perspective without undue influence from her spouse until she was forced to face him again.

The plan went awry the moment the glass door opened, Sebastian walked into the shower and moved behind her, as if he had a standing invitation.

His audacity momentarily stunned her into silence. Yet when he reached around her and grasped the bottle of shampoo from the mosaic tile shelf, she spun on him, putting herself in close proximity to a very naked, very virile, very *stimulated* man. "Do you mind?"

He took a quick sniff before placing some of the liquid in his palm. "I do not mind at all. In fact, I like the lavender. Now turn around."

She gathered all the reasons to resist him. Reasons that had ironically kept him from her over the past few months. "You may turn around and leave."

"Not until I wash your hair."

That would qualify as an unusual request. "Why?"

"Could you humor me, please?"

She caught the faint scent of alcohol. "Are you intoxicated?"

"Only with your beauty."

Clearly the liquor was speaking for him. "I smell scotch."

"I might have had a drink. Or two."

"I consider that inadvisable in light of your fatigue."

"I'm not too exhausted or too mashed to wash your hair. In fact, it would be an honor to do it. And I promise you will enjoy it."

Granted, she would, though she wondered who had kidnapped her stoic husband and replaced him with this considerate clone. She mulled the offer over a few minutes and surrendered to the prospect of pleasure— with one concession. "Oh, all right. But only if you will leave after you are finished."

"Agreed."

Nasira faced the tiled wall again and attempted to feign indifference. Yet when Sebastian slid his hands into her hair and began to massage her scalp, she practically melted against him. "That feels exquisite," she murmured.

Sebastian brushed a kiss across her cheek. "You deserve to feel that way. I recognize I've neglected my duties and haven't exactly been a doting husband."

She had never expected him to be doting, yet she did approve of this version of Sebastian. Then suddenly his hands drifted from her hair to her shoulders and came to rest on her breasts. Odd how he had not touched her in six months and now, as if someone had snapped on a sexual light switch, the former version of her husband had returned.

"You are exquisite," he murmured as he pressed against her bottom.

"You are a cad."

"Henry is the cad. I have no control over him."

Nasira stifled a laugh. "I have always wondered what would possess a man to name a cherished part of his anatomy after his prized horse."

He winked. "It's quite logical because that horse is a premiere stallion."

She elbowed him in the ribs. "Since you are finished

washing my hair, I need to rinse out the shampoo and you need to vacate the premises."

Against her better judgment, she turned her back to him, stepped beneath the flowing water and soaked her hair, giving Sebastian complete access to her body. He took supreme advantage of her vulnerable position by running his palms down her torso, over the bend of her waist and on to her hips.

Regardless of her nagging need for him, Nasira side-stepped Sebastian and sent him a frustrated look. "You agreed that when you were finished, you would leave."

He took the blue washcloth folded on the shelf and added a small dollop of gel. "I'm not finished yet."

Unable to move, Nasira watched as Sebastian washed her body, beginning with her shoulders and arms before he moved down to her breasts, and then her belly. He knelt and bathed each of her legs gently, all the while smiling up at her until he straightened. His crystal blue eyes seemed to darken as he shifted his attention to between her thighs. He lingered there for a time, teasing slightly, setting her on edge before he stepped back and draped the washcloth over the chrome rack to his left.

"There you go," he said. "Clean as a whistle."

"Why are you doing this, Sebastian?"

His eyes looked a bit hazy now. "Because I want you to relax. I'm certain you will sleep much better now."

Not very likely. Not when she still wanted him in every way. "I am onto you, Sebastian."

He attempted an innocent expression. "I'm sure I do not know what you mean."

"Yes, you do. However, you can attempt to seduce

me from dawn to dusk but we will still remain at an impasse."

"I was simply trying to be considerate." He grabbed the bottle of gel and began lathering his body. "Granted, a dawn-to-dusk seduction sounds interesting. Perhaps we shall try that in the near future."

"I'm going to bed now," she said as she quickly rinsed off without looking at him.

"I will join you shortly."

"I'll make you a nice place on the rug."

"I so cherish being treated like the family hound."

She sent him a quelling look as she opened the glass door. "We agreed on that arrangement."

He gave her a half smile. "Spoilsport."

As usual, he glossed over the seriousness of their situation with wit and sarcasm. Angry with him, and herself, Nasira left the shower, dried off, wrapped the towel around her and tucked it closed between her breasts. She then twisted her hair into a braid, brushed her teeth and returned to the bedroom, leaving Sebastian alone to finish his shower.

In the past, she would have crawled into bed without clothes but decided with her husband in the house, it would be best to dress in a short blue gown, as if donning silk armor. Of course, if Sebastian sneaked beneath the sheets in the middle of the night, the negligee wouldn't provide any real protection.

Protection. He would not attempt consummation without any form of birth control. He had made that quite clear earlier. In that case, she supposed she could be benevolent and allow him into the bed.

She questioned the wisdom of that reasoning when Sebastian entered the room, a thick white towel slung low on his hips. Even after all their years together, even after seeing him completely nude in the shower a few minutes ago, the sight of his lean swimmer's physique still took her breath away. Many nights she had explored all the masculine planes and valleys, at first under his tutelage, until she had learned exactly how to touch him and kiss him. She had possessed a certain power over him during those times. She dearly wanted to experience that now...

"Sira, are you all right?"

Startled into reality, Nasira averted her eyes and shook off the recollections, though she could not shake the heat. "I am tired."

"As am I," he said as he approached the bed. "So exhausted I could sleep on the floor. Oh, that's right. I'm supposed to do that very thing."

Nasira pulled back the comforter and pointed to the opposite side of the mattress. "I am willing to take pity on you as long as you maintain a wide berth between us."

He grinned. "You are most generous, my lady. And I promise I will be the perfect gentleman."

If only she could believe that. "I will hold you to that promise."

As Nasira slid beneath the covers, her husband returned to the bathroom then came back without the towel or any clothes whatsoever. "Could you possibly put something on, Sebastian?"

He frowned as he climbed into bed beside her.

"Sweetheart, you know I prefer to have nothing on when I sleep. So do you."

"We are guests in this house."

He rolled onto his back and stacked his hands behind his head. "I highly doubt Rafe or Violet will do a bed check to make certain we're appropriately dressed."

That led Nasira to another question. "What did you and my brother discuss tonight?"

He continued to stare at the ceiling. "The strange ways of women and the complete ignorance of men."

"Be serious."

"I am."

"Then please explain."

"At times women say one thing, then do another, while most men are painfully honest. You'd rather spend a day shopping and men would rather engage in sports. Women want to discuss their feelings. Men would rather discuss something as dull as the weather to avoid that at all costs."

"The last part is definitely accurate," she muttered.

"Perhaps that's because we don't necessarily have deep feelings."

"Or at least those you care to share."

Too weary to continue the conversation, Nasira turned off the lamp and turned her back to her spouse. "Good night, Sebastian."

"Sleep well, Sira."

If only she could. For at least an hour, maybe more, Nasira tossed and turned, well aware that her naked husband was very near...and deep in throes of slumber, as evidenced by his steady breathing.

Little by little Nasira began to drift off and soon found herself immersed in an erotic state when Sebastian's hand drifted to her breast. She reveled in the intimate stroking between her thighs. Once more she was captive to his skill and to her own sexuality. Another orgasm—the second one tonight—claimed her with remarkable force. Before the climax had completely calmed, Sebastian moved atop her then eased inside her. Steady thrusts, ragged breaths, undeniable mutual desire…

He whispered her name and she stroked his hair, as if nothing bad had ever transpired between them.

Then suddenly awareness dawned of what they were doing, and what they hadn't done. "Sebastian," she said in a harsh whisper. "We have to stop."

When Sebastian tensed and shuddered, she recognized she had been too late with the warning.

After he finally rolled away, Nasira waited for his reaction and wondered if he was even aware of what had transpired. She received her answer when he sighed, sat up and muttered, "Bloody hell, what have we done?"

She snapped the light on and studied his profile. "Apparently we had unprotected sex."

He shot her a borderline distressed look. "Apparently."

"This is not all my fault, Sebastian. I told you to sleep on the rug."

"You offered me the bed."

"You did not have to accept."

"You shouldn't be so sexy."

"You should have foregone the liquor."

He raked a hand through his tousled hair. "It's clearly futile to blame each other or concern ourselves with the consequences. What's done is done."

"If you are concerned about pregnancy, I was off the pill for almost a year before I conceived the last time. It is highly unlikely that would happen again after only one time."

He appeared skeptical. "Unlikely but not impossible."

Normally Nasira would be happy to know she might finally have a baby, but not with such serious problems still looming over them. "Would it be so horrible if I happened to be pregnant?"

After punching his pillow twice, Sebastian shifted onto his side, keeping his back to her. "That's a discussion for another day."

"A discussion we need to have very soon, Sebastian."

"Would you prefer I move to the floor?" he asked after a few seconds of silence, reverting back to the man who refused to have any semblance of a meaningful conversation.

She preferred he stop clamming up. "It's too late to concern ourselves about that now."

"Then good night, Sira."

"Good night, Sebastian."

As she stared at the ceiling, Nasira wondered how she could feel so bereft after making love with her husband. It was as if they'd returned to the days before she had left London—she was suspended in a state of emotional gridlock with a spouse who constantly erected emotional walls. Could they get past the standoff? In the morning she would decide once and for all if finding out would be worth the potential heartache.

Three

Nasira awoke to an empty space beside her and a strong sense of regret. She could only imagine what Sebastian was thinking. She wouldn't be surprised if he had already summoned the pilot of his posh corporate jet and flown back to London.

After showering and seeing to her morning routine, she dressed in white slacks and a sleeveless blue blouse, slid her feet into silver sandals and started downstairs to see if he had indeed left. When she heard the sound of two familiar male voices, she acknowledged she had been wrong in her assumptions, at least for the moment.

She reached the bottom landing, crossed the parlor and headed into the kitchen to find her husband and brother seated at the built-in banquette, having coffee together. They both quickly stood, looking as if they were errant schoolboys caught in a prank.

"Good morning, darling," Sebastian said, taking her aback with his friendly tone. "Sleep well?"

She didn't know if he was playing at being clueless or he didn't remember what had happened between them. "I slept well enough."

"Good because we have a busy day planned, thanks to Rafe."

Nasira leveled her gaze on her brother. "What does that mean?"

"I will let Sebastian explain," Rafe said as he started toward the parlor. "At the moment, I have to accompany Violet to speak with the caterer."

With that, he rushed away, leaving Nasira alone with her husband. "I find it difficult to believe my brother would involve you in the wedding plans, so I assume we're not expected to meet with the caterer."

"You would be correct. I asked Rafe to find us suitable lodging and he has the perfect place."

"Us?"

"Yes."

"I never agreed to that."

He gestured toward the chair Rafe had vacated. "Please sit so we can discuss this."

"Yes, let's." She settled in to the seat and waited for him to continue.

"Would you like coffee? Or perhaps tea?" he asked.

"I would like orange juice." And an explanation for why he clearly believed she would want to cohabitate with him, especially after his attitude last night.

He rose from the chair and walked to the refrigerator to retrieve the orange juice, poured her a glass and set it on the wooden table. He then took the chair opposite her and folded his hands before him. "I realize you left London to escape me, or perhaps our problems, but I am not willing to toss in the towel until we have explored all alternatives to remaining apart indefinitely."

Neither was she, though she understood they might never be able to compromise on the issue of having children. They never would unless he decided to actually discuss it. "You believe the only way we can do that would be to live under the same roof?"

"Yes, I do."

She had her doubts. "I know you, Sebastian. You will not tolerate a simple hotel room, and I do not believe you'll find a penthouse suite anywhere near Royal. If I decide to do this, I refuse to reside too far away from Rafiq and Violet."

"You're right, but there are houses available."

She suffered the second shock of the morning. "You purchased a house?"

He shook his head. "No. Rafe knows a man who is willing to open his home to us while he and the family travel abroad."

Living in a stranger's house did not seem like a favorable option. "What man?"

"His name is Sheikh Darin Shakir. I believe he hails from a country close to your homeland."

She had heard the name bandied about by Mac. "I know of him. In fact, his reputation precedes him."

Sebastian frowned. "In what way?"

"He killed a man several years ago."

"He's a bloody murderer?"

She gained some satisfaction from shocking her husband this time. "Actually, it is my understanding his love interest was being held captive by this criminal, forcing him to shoot the evildoer to save her life. Although I despise violence, I find the concept of coming to a woman's rescue somewhat romantic."

"I find resorting to murder somewhat disturbing." Sebastian sat back and sighed. "Perhaps we should explore other avenues."

"It's past history, Sebastian. He is very well respected and in fact married to the woman he saved. They have several children."

"Are you absolutely certain the man is safe? I refuse to put you in harm's way."

"As I've said, he is a hero in the town's eyes. I also know my brother would never send me into a dangerous situation."

Sebastian slapped his palms on the table and stood. "Then it's settled. We shall go meet this knight in tainted armor and see if the house passes muster. We need to hurry since they will be leaving shortly after lunch for the trip."

She refused to rush into the decision to join him. "I still have qualms about living together at this point in time."

"What qualms?"

"First of all, although I came here to confront Rafe, I also intended to have time away from you to think."

"On the contrary, last night you wanted to talk."

He did present a valid point. "Yes, but I'm not certain you would be willing to do that."

He rested his hand on the back of her chair. "If we decide the accommodations are suitable, I will strike a bargain with you."

Always the negotiator. "Go on."

"If you will give me one week and the arrangement doesn't suit you, or if I don't meet your expectations, then you are free to leave and I will return to the UK."

She mulled the proposition over a moment and decided that it did seem fair. After all, she truly wanted to attempt to mend the relationship if at all possible. "All right. I will agree to your terms."

"Great. Our chariot awaits."

She pushed back from the table and came to her feet. "I wouldn't consider that truck a chariot."

"I had another vehicle delivered this morning from Dallas. One that is more suitable. You'll see when I bring it around."

"Believe it or not, I find that somewhat disappointing."

He pushed a lock of hair behind her ear, a habit he had established from the first night they had met. "Why is that?"

"Sedans do not have beds."

Noting the look of sheer surprise on Sebastian's handsome face, she turned to retrieve her purse and sunglasses, smiling all the way upstairs and back down again. Perhaps she should not be encouraging her husband in a sexual sense, yet she could not seem to resist the desire his presence had resurrected. The ever present need.

If they had to exist in close quarters, she should make the best of their time together for however long it might last. If they jointly decided their marriage was over, she would make more memories to carry with her to override the bad.

If luck prevailed, the Shakirs' family home would be a happy place perfect for new beginnings.

"This isn't a house, it's a fortress."

Nasira tore her gaze away from the massive white stone structure to glance at Sebastian. "And this veritable limousine you've leased goes quite well with it."

He sent her a half smile. "It's a Jaguar, Sira. Only the best for my bride."

She didn't bother to ask how he had acquired it simply because she did not care. She only cared about meeting the mysterious man who resided in the residence. And of course, the woman who had been worthy of his rescue.

As soon as Sebastian pulled to a stop beneath the portico, a dark-haired, dark-skinned man dressed in black shirt and slacks emerged from the double iron doors. Nasira recognized him from the photograph she had seen at the Texas Cattleman's Club—Darin Shakir, sheikh extraordinaire.

He opened her door and greeted her with an intense look and a guarded smile. "Mrs. Edwards."

"Sheikh Shakir," she said as she slid out of the luxury sedan. "It is a pleasure to finally meet you."

"The pleasure is mine," he said with a nod.

Sebastian rounded the hood and offered his hand to Darin. "I truly appreciate your offer, Sheikh Shakir."

"You may call me Darin," he replied. "I have never embraced my royal status."

Nasira had also learned that about him, which could explain how he had settled in a place like Texas. Then again, so had her brother.

Darin showed them into the house where they were met by an attractive woman with red spiraling curls and bright green eyes. "Welcome to our home, you two. I'm Fiona Shakir."

"I am Nasira Edwards, and this is my husband, Sebastian," she said, beating her spouse to the punch.

At that moment, three dark-haired little boys entered the room and stood between the Shakirs like miniature soldiers. "These are our sons," Darin said. "Halim, Kalib and Samir."

Fiona rested her palm on the youngest one's head. "Otherwise known as Hal, who's ten, Kal, eight, and Sam, five."

The pitter-patter of footsteps echoed in the marble entryway, drawing everyone's attention to the little girl dashing into the foyer, her auburn-tinted curls bouncing in time with her gait. She immediately threw her arms around Darin's legs, leading him to sweep her up. "And this is Liana, our youngest," Darin said. "She will be three years old in three months."

When the little girl touched her father's face, and the stoic sheikh gave his daughter the softest look, Nasira's heart melted. "You have a beautiful family."

Fiona patted her belly. "Thank you, and in about five months, we'll be expanding it with another boy."

Nasira experienced a sense of awe and a slight sting of envy. "Four boys should be interesting."

"Very interesting," Sebastian said. "How do you manage caring for so many children?"

Fiona slid her arm around Darin's waist. "With a lot of love and sharing."

"And our nanny, Amelia," Darin added.

"A part-time nanny," Fiona amended. "When Amelia isn't here, I've learned to be extremely organized out of self-defense. Otherwise the house will be utter chaos and I'll be a raving maniac."

Darin pointed behind him. "Boys, return to the play-room." No sooner than he commanded it, the Shakir sons departed.

Fiona gestured toward the hall beyond the foyer. "Come inside and I'll show you around."

"I would enjoy seeing the livestock," Sebastian said to Darin. "We can leave the wives to tour the house and talk about us when we're out of earshot."

Darin finally smiled. "I would be glad to show you the stables."

"Take Liana with you," Fiona said. "She'll throw a fit if you walk outside without her."

Sebastian looked somewhat alarmed. "Is it wise to take a child around the horses?"

Fiona smiled. "She's fine as long as she's super-vised."

Darin shifted Liana from one hip to the other. "We

have several Arabians if you and your wife would like to ride."

"It would be a pleasure," Sebastian began, "yet I'm afraid my wife would probably balk at the idea."

But Sebastian was wrong. "I would love nothing more than to go for a ride. I spent much of my youth on the back of a horse."

Sebastian frowned. "You've never told me that in our ten years together."

"You never asked."

"Ten years?" Fiona interjected as if she sensed the tension. "Darin and I have been married that long. Do you two have children?"

Nasira swallowed around the nagging lump in her throat. "Not yet."

"We have a very busy life in London," Sebastian added. "And we both enjoy traveling. Nasira is involved in charity work and my shipping business requires quite a bit of time."

Fiona shrugged. "Children are definitely time-con-suming."

"And wonderful," Nasira said, determined to get her point across to her husband. "I definitely want at least one or perhaps two."

Sebastian regarded Darin. "Shall we begin the tour of the stables? We wouldn't want to detain you in light of your upcoming vacation."

Leave it to her husband to avoid the topic of children. And that gave Nasira pause. "I am very much looking forward to seeing the rest of the house."

"Right this way," Fiona said as she gestured Nasira forward.

They made their way through a large formal lounge with gleaming dark wood floors and several seating areas containing multicolored leather furniture and assorted club chairs.

She already felt at home surrounded by such opulence. "This is very grand but comfortable."

"Thank you, Nasira." Fiona nodded toward the sweeping staircase. "We have five bedrooms upstairs and our other family room, which is always a mess. So I'll concentrate on the downstairs for now. But feel free to explore when you're here."

Provided they decided to stay there, though she had to admit she would love it. "We so appreciate your hospitality."

"You are so welcome," Fiona said as she took off at a fast clip. "The two guest bedrooms are down here."

Nasira admired the luxury of the first bedroom Fiona showed her. It was accented in whites and grays with a plush king bed and gorgeous en suite bath. The second was equally remarkable though the color palette featured differing shades of blue. Nasira welcomed the fact that if serious conflicts arose during their time her, she could have one room and Sebastian could have the other.

"Amelia usually stays in one these rooms when she spends the night," Fiona began, "but we're taking her with us. Darin and I could use a little alone time, if you catch my drift."

Nasira was not familiar with the term, yet she did understand the meaning behind it. "I have no doubt enjoying private moments with your husband must be difficult in light of the children's needs."

The redhead grinned and winked. "We women have needs too."

Something Nasira had realized all too well last night. "Yes, we do."

Fiona led her out into the corridor and waved her forward. "The housekeeper, Annie, will be in every day if you decide to stay with us. And she prepares wonderful meals."

"That would not be necessary."

"I insist," Fiona said as she stopped in the great room. "Besides, Annie would be lost if she didn't have something to do. I promise she won't be in the way. In fact, you won't even know she's here most of the time."

A phantom maid was quite a novel idea. "Well I would not want her to feel unwanted."

"I can show you our bedroom if you'd like," Fiona began, "or we can take a look at the kitchen."

"I would love to see the nursery," Nasira blurted without thought.

"Then follow me."

They crossed to the opposite end of the house and walked down another long hall until Fiona paused at a door with a keypad. "This is the elevator to the upper floor. I'll leave the code in case you need it."

She could not imagine why they would. "Did I not see a staircase?"

"Yes, you did." Fiona smiled as they continued on side by side at a much slower pace. "We use it to get to the second floor fast if one of the kids needs us during the night. Darin is usually the one who hops out of bed first. He's a very light sleeper."

"How did the two of you meet?" Nasira asked, overcome with curiosity.

"In a Vegas lounge," Fiona said. "I happened to be bartending when he walked in and he thought I was someone else."

"Someone else?"

"Yes. An FBI agent. It's a long story but let's just say that particular night started a harrowing adventure that led to this wonderful life full of love and chaos and beautiful children. And speaking of children, this is where the babies stay."

Fiona opened the double doors to a large nursery that Nasira could only describe as a children's wonderland. A majestic white canopy crib draped in sheer pale green netting to complement the gender-neutral decor had been positioned between two windows. Stuffed animals of all shapes and sizes dotted built-in shelves that also held trinkets and framed photos of the Shakir children at various points of their life. It was a remarkable place that indicated a very happy family lived here.

Fiona pointed to a small bed to their right. "Liana still sleeps there for the time being. We'll move her upstairs to the big girl room right before the baby comes. At least that's the plan. I'm not sure how well her daddy is going to take not having her nearby."

Nasira could see where that might be an issue. "They seem to be very close."

"She's definitely a daddy's girl. You'll figure that one out if you and Sebastian have a daughter."

Regret and memories washed over Nasira as she walked to the crib and ran her hand over the soft coral blanket folded at the end of the mattress. How many times had she imagined her own baby in such a precious bed? How many times had she cried over the end of that dream? Her hand automatically came to rest on her abdomen, and then the familiar tears arrived as sudden as a summer rain. Unwelcome tears that she could not seem to control.

She felt a hand on her shoulder. "Nasira, are you okay?"

Not in the least. She turned around and sniffed. "I had a miscarriage six months ago. It was early in the pregnancy but still no less devastating."

Fiona snapped a tissue from the box on the changing table and handed it to her. "I'm so sorry, Nasira, and I can relate."

She dabbed at her eyes. "You can?"

"Like you, I had a first trimester miscarriage between Kal and Sam. It broke my heart."

Finally, someone who could understand and perhaps provide insight. "How did Darin react to the loss?"

Fiona shrugged. "He was extremely supportive even though he didn't touch me for a couple of months. I think he worried I might break."

"Sebastian avoided me for six months."

Fiona's green eyes went wide. "You haven't made love since you lost the baby?"

Nasira felt the urge to confess, yet thought it best not to reveal too much. "That was the case until last night, although I am still in a quandary over how it happened. In fact, the whole evening was rather odd."

"I'd think you would be relieved," Fiona said. "Six months is a long time without making whoopee."

"True, but Sebastian's behavior was completely out of character. First of all, he arrived at Rafiq's house uninvited and punched Mac McCallum because he believed we were having some sort of tryst, which is absolutely absurd."

Fiona gasped. "He did not!"

"He did. I was completely shocked by his behavior yet admittedly somewhat attracted to his sudden show of machismo. Sebastian is usually so controlled."

Fiona chuckled. "I know exactly what you mean because Darin is like that, too. But there's no shame in wanting to jump his bones after he defended your honor, even if he mistakenly thought you were fooling around."

Nasira had definitely wanted him, yet she had never been the aggressor in the relationship. "For the sake of accuracy, I was not exactly looking to rekindle our love life at that moment. Yet he convinced me to have dinner with him and then he virtually seduced me in the ridiculously large pickup truck he rented."

"Welcome to Texas, girlfriend. Sex in a pickup truck is practically a sport."

Nasira couldn't contain her smile. "That actually came later, in the middle of the night, after Sebastian had two toddies on top of his jet lag." She sighed. "You must think I am a complete dolt, telling you all the sordid details."

Fiona folded her arms across her middle. "Hey, I'm

a good listener, and it's sure not stupid to want to make love to your husband."

Then why did she feel so foolish? "I should not want him after what he has done. Or what he has not done. Not only did he avoid lovemaking, any serious communication between us has been at a complete standstill. He refuses to talk about our loss or how he feels about it."

"Darin isn't a great communicator, either," Fiona said. "But I can't imagine him completely shutting down and if he does try that, I have ways to make him talk."

"Sebastian has not only shut down, he acts as if he no longer wants children. Maybe he never has. In fact, I had to stop taking…" She had already revealed too much. Said too much. "Again, I do apologize for burdening you with my problems."

"Burden away, Nasira. We're members of the miscarriage club and it's not a good club to join."

"No, it is not."

Fiona's face took on a serious expression. "If you don't mind me asking, do you know why your husband suddenly changed his mind about being a father?"

This would be the most difficult part to explain. "Actually, we met and married very quickly and we never actually discussed it at length. I did know that his father and stepmother were adamant that he produce an heir because he is an only child, so I mistakenly assumed we would eventually have children. Yet it took years before we finally conceived." With some regrettable deception on her part.

"If he doesn't change his mind, what are you going to do?"

"I have no clue at this point in time." And she really didn't.

Fiona patted her cheek. "Stick to your guns, Nasira. It's one thing if both parties don't want a baby, but it's another thing if one does and one doesn't. Regardless, I hope you both work it out."

So did Nasira. "That's why we are here. I initially came to Royal to check up on my brother and gain some space, yet Sebastian insisted on following me. We have both agreed to try to compromise. Hopefully, opening your home to us will aid in that goal."

"It's a magical place," Fiona said with a grin. "But just another bit of friendly advice. If he has sex on his mind, don't make it easy for him until you know you're both on the same page when it comes to the future. If he doesn't want to talk, then give him a little nudge."

If only she had mastered that tack. "What do you suggest?"

"Be a seductress, but play hard to get to get what you need. Eventually you'll have him eating out of your hand."

"Would that not make me a tease?"

"Sometimes we have to resort to desperate measures, Nasira. Playing cat and mouse always drives Darin insane, and I guess that's why we have so many kids."

They shared in a laugh and a surprising embrace before Fiona said, "Let's go see if the men have come in from the stables."

Nasira felt she should express her gratitude again.

"Let's. And please know how much I appreciate your candor and comradeship. You have bolstered my optimism."

"No problem, Nasira. We girls have just got to stick together."

The sound of feminine laughter filtered into the chef's kitchen, leading Sebastian to believe the two wives must be getting along famously. He couldn't exactly say the same when it came to his connection to Darin Shakir. The man spoke in brief sentences and appeared to be incapable of smiling, unless it was directed at his daughter. However, he had been a polite host during their tour of the stables, right down to pointing out where Sebastian should step to prevent ruining his Italian loafers.

As Nasira moved into the room, chatter went on around him but he tuned it out and focused on watching his wife. Even after all the years they'd spent together, Sebastian still found her grace and beauty breathtaking. He liked the way she kept her slender hands in motion when she spoke. He liked the way her dark eyes lit up when she laughed. He truly relished her breasts that were unfortunately concealed by her black hair falling in soft waves, crimped from the braid she'd worn to bed last night. He imagined those silken locks on his chest, along with her soft lips, moving down his belly and lower....

"Can I get you anything, Sebastian?"

He brought his attention to Fiona to find her sport-

ing an odd look. "I could use a glass of water." Mainly
to pour down his shorts to preserve his dignity.

"Would you like one too, Nasira?" she asked.

His wife frowned at him as if she had channeled his
dirty thoughts. "No, thank you. I suppose Sebastian and
I should take our leave so we can discuss your wonderful offer for us to stay in your home."

Darin stepped forward, the toddler still on his hip.
"We will give you your privacy while we return to our
packing. If you decide to stay, we will provide you with
the key and the gate code so you may return at your
leisure."

Fiona set a glass of water on the marble island next to
Sebastian. "Liana, tell Mr. and Mrs. Edwards goodbye."

After Darin set the little girl on her feet, she immediately rushed to Sebastian and wrapped her arms around
his legs. "Bye, bye, Mr. Man."

Seeing the grin on the child's face sent a spear of
regret through Sebastian. He ruffled her dark hair and
returned her smile. "Goodbye, Princess Liana. I am
grateful to have met you and your noble steed, Puddles."

Her grin widened as she moved to Nasira and took
her hand. "Bye, bye, pretty lady."

Nasira knelt at her level and touched the girl's face.
"Goodbye, little princess. Have a wonderful time on
your trip."

Fiona stepped forward and took Liana's hand. "Take
your time, you two. When you're ready, just press the
button that says *family room* on the wall by the stove
and we'll come running."

After the couple disappeared around the corner, Sebastian faced Sira again. "Well, what do you think of the place?"

"I think it is very lovely."

"Not too shabby, I suppose."

"I also think your reaction to Liana was lovely as well."

He should have seen that coming. "She's a very interesting child though somewhat chatty. She is quite enamored of her pony."

"She seemed somewhat enamored of you."

"She is simply friendly." And he simply needed to divert Nasira's attention from the topic before she forced him to revisit his decision not to have a child. "By the way, there's a spa on the deck next to the pool. That alone would persuade me to stay."

"I cannot recall if Elsa packed my swimsuit."

"Elsa never forgets a thing. And on the off chance she did, we will swim in the nude."

She averted her eyes. "Keep your voice down, Sebastian."

Her innocence had come out of hiding. "Why? I assume this couple knows about all things sexual considering they are well on their way to creating an entire rugby team."

That earned him her smile and a wistful look. "You are so amusing. They have a wonderful family. They are quite lucky to have each other."

He realized how strongly his wife had been affected by the children. Children he could not offer her at the moment. Nevertheless, he hoped to come up with a plan that he would present later. Much later. "Are you still willing to reside here with me until the end of the week?"

"Yes, with a few conditions," she said.

He should have seen that coming. "And what would those be?"

"First, we stay in separate suites."

Bloody hell. "Why?"

"Because we need to concentrate on our relationship without any complications that will cloud our judgment."

Double bloody hell. "If you are referring to sex, you must admit that has always worked well between us. Why would we want to exclude that from our time together?"

She barked out a cynical laugh. "I find that somewhat ironic considering that until last night, you refused to sleep with me in every sense of the word for the past six months."

He couldn't provide an explanation without baring his soul completely. He had been taught by his father early in life that men did not give in to emotions. "I was simply allowing you to recover completely."

"Have you forgotten what happened last night when you were in my bed?"

"Actually, I barely remember it." Unfortunately.

"You do remember the birth control issue, correct?"

He had attempted to forget that, yet the possible consequences still haunted him. "Yes, I remember."

"Well, nothing has changed in that regard. We still do not have any protection against pregnancy."

Not yet, but he intended to rectify that with a trip

to the market. And perhaps he would pick up a box of chocolates along with the condoms. "I see your point, and I agree to your terms." For the time being.

"Second condition," she continued. "You must promise you will engage in meaningful conversations and answer my questions with candor without any comedy."

That would be somewhat difficult. "I promise I will try, as long as you promise to be patient."

"I will agree to those terms."

Simple enough. "Then I suppose we should tell the Shakirs we will be accepting their hospitable invitation."

Sebastian could only hope that agreeing to her terms would not prove to be his downfall.

Four

Later that afternoon, when they returned to the Shakirs' house, luggage in hand, they found a note on the door from the owners inviting them to enjoy their home, and lunch awaiting them.

After Sebastian keyed in the code to allow them entry, Nasira started for the guest wing with her husband trailing behind her. She paused in the hallway to turn and almost ran into a wall of masculine chest. "Which room do you prefer?"

"The one where you'll be staying."

She sighed and stepped back. "We've already discussed this, Sebastian. Until we have our issues settled, I insist we adhere to our initial plan."

"I am only being honest at your request."

And infuriating. "I will take the suite on the right

and you can take the one across the hall. I assure you, they are both very nice. I will meet you in the kitchen after I have settled in."

"Yes, dear."

Relieved her husband had not put up much of a fight, Nasira entered the blue suite and set her suitcase and garment bag on the bench at the end of the bed. She quickly hung her dresses in the huge closet and put away her other clothes in the bureau, then returned to the corridor to find it deserted. Without waiting for Sebastian, she immediately left for the great room, all the while reflecting on his interaction with little Liana. He seemed quite charmed by the toddler, and perhaps that meant there could still be hope for their marriage yet. Or perhaps it had only been a show for the proud parents.

When she reached the kitchen, Nasira found a spread of luscious salads, cheeses, breads and cold cuts laid out on the informal dinette set against a large picture window that revealed a remarkable view of the countryside.

"It certainly looks appetizing."

She turned to find her husband standing close by, hands in pockets. "It looks wonderful. All of it. The food. The pastureland. The pool and the spa. We might as well be staying at a resort."

He raked back a chair, sat and then rubbed his hands together. "Personally I could consume most of this."

She claimed the seat across from him. "Please let me have a bit before you take it all."

He winked. "Sweetheart, although I would like it all, I will take what you will give me."

She could so easily walk into his lair but remembered

Fiona's advice. She would play along for now before she would play hard to get. "I promise I will give you enough to keep you sated."

He appeared pleasantly surprised by her response. "I look forward to it."

As they dined, a heavy fog of tension hung over them. A palpable tension long absent from their lives. Nasira held tight to her goal to persuade him to talk about issues he had always suppressed. During this time together, she vowed to learn as much as she could about the man she had lived with for a decade, and she would do whatever that required.

"I found Fiona Shakir to be quite friendly," she said, breaking the silence.

"And clearly quite fertile."

"Would you please stop deriding her for choosing to have children?"

He pushed aside his empty plate. "I'm not deriding her. I'm simply stating the obvious."

Nasira opted for a change of subject. "What should we do this afternoon?"

His smile arrived as slowly as the sunrise. "I know what I would like to do for the remainder of the day."

Stay strong, Nasira. "I would like to hear your plans, as long as they involve remaining vertical."

"I'd say that's altogether possible and in my opinion, preferable during a lengthy ride."

Images of being taken against a wall plagued her. "Need I remind you of our agreement?"

He rubbed his chin. "I do not readily recall any clause prohibiting horseback riding."

She tossed her napkin at him and he caught it in one hand. "You cad."

"Cad? What did you think I meant?"

She pushed back from the table and stood. "Do not play ignorant, Sebastian. Since you've arrived, every time you open your mouth, innuendo spills out."

He had the gall to grin. "Perhaps you only assume that because you're having naughty sex thoughts."

That only heightened her irritation. "If that were the case, could you blame me?"

He released a rough sigh. "No, I suppose I couldn't. You have been greatly deprived, with the exception of last night. However, I would like to make up for that now if you will allow it."

She refused to give in so easily. "I appreciate the gesture, but you will have to make up for my deprivation without any expectations in regard to lovemaking."

He pushed the chair back, came to his feet and executed a bow. "My lady, I would be honored if you would join me for an equestrian adventure, and I promise no clothes will be shed."

She could not help but smile. "Yes, I will join you. And speaking of clothes, I will need to change into something more suitable."

He slapped his forehead with his palm. "I didn't bring anything but slacks and loafers."

"Then perhaps we should find something else to do."

"No, I'll travel into town to purchase appropriate clothing. Or perhaps I should say I'll mosey into town."

"Is it worth that much effort?"

He walked up to her and kissed her cheek. "*You* are

worth the effort. And I need to pick up a few more items that will benefit us both."

Before Nasira could respond, Sebastian strode out of the kitchen, leaving her standing there, pondering what he had up his sleeve. She would simply have to wait and see.

Nasira waited for what seemed to be infinity for Sebastian to return, until her patience began to wane. Dressed in designer jeans and fashionable boots, she located the path that led to the pasture and made her way to the stable. She soon came upon a large white rock structure surrounded by paddocks that held grazing mares and a few precious foals. It appeared everything about the ranch fostered new life and that only fed her melancholy.

When she entered the barn, Nasira found a lengthy aisle lined with stalls, mostly empty until she reached the end of the line where a beautiful bay stuck its head out of the top of the door.

She cautiously approached to measure the horse's reaction to her appearance. When she held out her hand and began stroking the thin white blaze between its eyes, she immediately received a soft nicker.

"Can I help you, ma'am?"

In response the unfamiliar voice, she turned her head to the right and spotted an older man with white-streaked hair peeking out from beneath his black baseball cap, whiskers scattered about his careworn face. She offered a smile and her hand. "I am Nasira Edwards, the Shakirs' houseguest."

His face relaxed as he gave her hand a hearty shake. "Oh, yeah. I met your husband earlier. He told me the two of you might be wantin' to take a ride today."

"And you are?"

He raked off his cap and grinned. "I forgot my manners. I'm Hadley Monroe but most people call me Cappy. I prefer that."

An odd name but a very cheerful man. "It is a pleasure to meet you, Cappy. I assume you work for the Shakirs."

He settled the cap back on his head. "Yes, ma'am. I take care of the livestock and my missus, Annie, keeps the house. That gelding you're scratchin' is Gus, or that's what I call him. He has some fancy name that's about a mile long."

She glanced at the mesmerized horse and smiled. "Do you live nearby?"

Cappy hooked a thumb over his shoulder. "If you go up those stairs back there, that leads to our place."

"Over the barn?"

He chuckled. "It's nicer than most people's houses. The nicest place I've ever lived in. Mr. Darin and Mrs. Fiona are good people."

"Yes they are."

The sound of footsteps drew Nasira's attention to the stable's entry to see a tall man striding down the aisle. She recognized the confident gait, the lean, toned body, the charming smile and handsome face. She did not recognize the chambray shirt rolled up at the sleeves, the jeans encasing those long legs or the cowboy boots covering his feet.

"Well, well," she said as he stopped before her. "Has there been a British invasion in the western store?"

Her husband's smile expanded. "As they say, when in Rome."

"Or Royal."

"I'm attempting to blend in. Do you not approve?"

She took a visual journey down his body and back up again. "Actually, I approve very much."

"I would think so since you seem to have an affinity for cowboys of late."

"Excuse me?"

"Your *friend*, Mac, the manhandling rancher."

The jealousy apparently had not abated, and that somewhat shocked Nasira, as well as aggravated her. "Oh, nonsense, Sebastian. Please get over that."

Without offering a rejoinder, Sebastian reached around her and stuck out his hand for a shake. "Nice to see you again, Cappy."

"Good to see you, too, Buck."

That turned Nasira around to face the grinning graying ranch hand. "Buck?"

"Cappy gives everyone a nickname," Sebastian said. "Isn't that right, Cappy?"

The older man touched the bill of his cap. "Yesiree, Buck. I call 'em like I see 'em."

Sebastian slid his arm around Nasira's waist. "What would you suggest for my wife?"

Cappy rubbed his chin for a few moments. "I can only think of one thing that fits. Beauty."

Sebastian laughed. "That would definitely fit."

Nasira felt heat rise from her throat to her face.

"Surely you can come up with something a bit more creative, Cappy."

The man grinned again. "Like I said, I call 'em like I see 'em. If you folks will excuse me, I'll go get Studly and bring him in so I can get back to work."

After Cappy left, Nasira faced her husband again. "Who is Studly?"

"Darin's stallion," Sebastian said. "His proper name is Knight something."

She had entered the land of strange names. "I would definitely prefer that to Studly."

"I'd prefer Studly to Buck."

Nasira could not help but smile. "Studly Edwards. It has a nice ring to it. Perhaps if we have a son we could use it."

Sebastian looked as if she had told him he had to sell the shipping business. "Darin told me to explore the path outside the back paddock. It leads to a nice creek," he said, changing the subject.

Of course he would avoid the topic of children. But as far as Nasira was concerned, they would be broaching that subject soon enough, and the discussion could determine their future.

Cappy returned leading a beautiful black Arabian with a large tooled saddle dotted with elaborate silver on his back. "Here ya go, Buck. He's ready to ride."

Sebastian frowned. "No English tack, I see."

"Nope," Cappy said. "But those prissy saddles aren't much different. This is just a bigger seat with a horn to hang on to. There's no need to bounce up and down unless you wanna do that."

The larger seat did not appear to be able to accommodate two people, which led Nasira to ask a question. "Will I have my own horse?"

"That fellow you've been scratchin' is all yours," Cappy said. "Gus will take good care of you. I'll get him tacked up and then you all can take off."

Nasira stood by as the ranch hand led Gus out of the stall and toward the rear of the barn. While she and Sebastian remained in the aisle, the stallion began to grow restless. "He appears to be rather spirited," she said. "Are you certain you can handle him?"

Sebastian scratched the horse's neck and that seemed to calm him somewhat. "If I can handle chasing a three-inch ball with mallet in hand on the back of a racing beast during a game of polo, I can manage one spirited stallion."

She had clearly dealt a blow to his ego. "Of course. How foolish of me to question your manhood."

"My manhood is never in question, sweetheart. You should know that after ten years."

"It is understandable I would have forgotten since I have had very limited exposure to your *manhood* for the past six months."

"Touché. Yet I do recall your manhood drought ending last night."

"Unfortunately I do not recall much about that at all, and neither do you, considering we were both half-asleep."

Cappy returned with the gelding, interrupting the banter and greatly embarrassing Nasira when she considered that he might have overheard. "They're all yours," he said. "Just go out the front, take a right and follow the trail past the back of the barn. Once you reach water, you're all out of path."

"Would we be allowed to explore the rest of the acreage, Cappy?" Sebastian asked.

The man chuckled. "Well, that would be close to two thousand acres, but if you want adventure, be my guest. Just take care not to get lost."

Nasira could imagine wandering around for days and days. "I believe we will stay on the path. My husband does not have the best sense of direction."

Sebastian sent her a quelling look. "Might I remind you that you have been known to become lost looking for the tube?"

"I have not."

"Yes, you have."

She suddenly remembered one incident from long ago. "For heaven's sake, Sebastian, that happened once right after we married and I barely knew my way around London."

Cappy cleared his throat. "I hate to interrupt, but I need to muck these stalls while you're gone. I'd like be done before midnight."

"Of course," Sebastian said. "Do you need assistance mounting your steed, Sira?"

She answered by putting her boot in the stirrup and hoisting herself onto the saddle. "No, I do not."

Sebastian laid a dramatic hand over his heart. "You wound me by not allowing me to make any show of chivalry."

She clasped the reins in one hand. "Knowing you

as well as I do, you only wanted an excuse to put your hand on my bum."

He frowned and mounted the stallion with ease. "Darling, you are going to lead our friend here to believe that I'm a scoundrel."

"If the moniker fits, *darling.*"

Cappy narrowed his eyes and studied them both. "How long have the two of you been hitched?"

"Ten years," they responded simultaneously.

"Well, that explains it," Cappy said. "Just some friendly advice. The missus and me have been married nearly forty years. In that time we figured out when you find yourself bickering a lot, the best way to cool down is taking a nekkid swim together in the crick. You should try it."

"Crick?" Sebastian asked.

Cappy scowled. "That's Texan for creek. See y'all when you get back."

With that, the man disappeared, leaving Nasira and Sebastian sitting atop the horses, staring at each other. And when her husband presented her with a slow, knowing grin, Nasira pointed at him despite the seductive images flashing in her mind. "Do not even think we will be engaging in that behavior."

He shrugged. "I can see some merit in the man's suggestion."

So could she. Bent on ignoring him and her own questionable thoughts, Nasira nudged the gelding forward with her heels, not bothering to look back.

When she guided Gus through the stable doors into the bright sunshine, Sebastian rode up to her side. "Perhaps you should lead the way since I have such a *terrible* sense of direction."

She turned right on the path without giving him a passing glance. "Could we call a truce and concentrate on having a pleasant ride?"

"I suppose I could do that. Will I be allowed to speak?"

She sent him a sideways glance. "I highly doubt I could prevent that if I tried."

"Your request is my command."

Whether he could be quiet for any real length of time remained to be seen, Nasira thought as they rode down the path at an easy pace.

As they traveled on, she relished the feel of the sun on her shoulders, the scent of freshly cut grass, the wide expanse of open land before them where livestock grazed nearby. "Oh, look," she said, breaking the silence. "A baby cow."

"I believe the proper term would be calf," Sebastian began," although that does conjure images of a disjointed leg frolicking in the field."

It took great effort to contain her laughter. "Always the witty one."

Another span of silence passed before Sebastian addressed her again. "When did you last communicate with your mother?"

The question came as a surprise to Nasira. "When I became pregnant."

She could feel his gaze boring into her. "Are you saying she doesn't know—"

"About the miscarriage? No."

"Why haven't you told her?"

"She did not share in my excitement over the pregnancy. She has never been concerned about my life."

He released a rough sigh. "I've never understood your hesitancy to reconnect with her."

"She does not welcome that, Sebastian. I remind her of my father."

"You are still her child."

"Perhaps, but I was raised by the palace staff. She only gave birth to me out of obligation."

"In a manner of speaking, I can relate. I'm certain that was the reasoning behind my birth. And that insistence on producing heirs is no bloody reason to bring a baby into this world. Nothing good can come of it."

"We are both good people, Sebastian."

"Good people whose mothers were forced to bring us into being."

Nasira saw an opportunity to encourage him to expand on his feelings. "Yet your mother loved you, did she not?"

"Yes, she did, until her untimely death."

A death that he had never discussed in detail in Nasira's presence, despite the fact she had asked numerous times during the beginning of her marriage. Eventually she had given up. "What exactly happened to her, Sebastian?"

His jaw tightened, a positive sign of anxiety. "She became ill."

That much she knew. "What did that illness involve?"

Sebastian shaded his eyes and focused on the horizon. "I believe I see the creek ahead."

Sebastian's behavior was a certain sign of emotional avoidance as far as Nasira was concerned. "I assume it must be painful to discuss the particulars, but I would like to know."

"It doesn't matter how or why. It only matters that she left her only son orphaned."

The comment gave Nasira pause. "Is that why you've avoided having a child of your own? Do you fear you will somehow desert them?"

"No. I've spent a lifetime having the importance of an heir crammed down my bloody throat."

Denial or not, Nasira sensed she had touched on the crux of his reluctance. "Have you ever considered the absolute joy fatherhood brings?"

He continued to stare straight ahead. "Most people I know pawn their children off on the nanny for the sake of their sanity."

Her husband was either terribly misguided or overly cynical. "Not the Shakirs. You would have realized that if you noticed the way Darin looked at his daughter."

"I noticed." Sebastian's tone was oddly laced with sadness.

Nasira wanted so badly to reach him. To uncover the secrets he harbored in his soul. "And you have no desire to experience that love?"

He attempted a smile that did not quite reach his eyes. "I desire to find out if Studly can fly."

When Sebastian and the stallion took off, Nasira remained behind for a few moments, pondering his need to escape. The behavior was so unlike Sebastian the businessman. As long as she had known him, he had always been a take-charge man. A man who had never avoided any challenges. A man who had been inclined to run from all things emotional.

Before her husband put too much physical distance between them, Nasira spurred the gelding into a gallop. She did not catch up to Sebastian until she reached the tree-lined ribbon of water where he had dismounted. She found him standing on the bank, the stallion's reins secured to a low-hanging limb. She climbed off Gus, tied him to the tree opposite Studly and went to Sebastian's side.

"Why do you always do that?" she asked when he didn't acknowledge her.

He picked up a stone and tossed it into the muddy green water. "I find speed exhilarating."

Her frustration over his evasion began to escalate. "That is not what I meant, Sebastian."

"I know."

The acknowledgment surprised her. "You promised me you would make an effort to be open about your feelings."

He finally faced her. "I would prefer to have a nice, relaxing afternoon with my wife, not to dredge up past history and events that cannot be changed. Could we possibly do that and leave the serious talk for a later time in a place that is not quite so serene?"

She recognized that her husband responded better with gentle persuasion. "All right. We shall postpone the conversation for the time being."

"I'm glad you see it my way."

When Sebastian took a seat on a large stump and

began to remove his boots and socks, Nasira worried he had other activities in mind. "Surely you are not going to take Cappy's suggestion about going swimming naked in the creek."

He glanced at her and winked. "I will if you will."

"I will not." Though admittedly she would under better circumstances.

"I thought as much," he said as he rolled up his pants legs. "Never fear, my dear. I'm only going to put my feet in the water. Would you care to join me?"

Nasira eyed the muddy green stream and wondered what lurked beneath. "Should we be afraid of reptiles and man-eating fish?"

Sebastian stood and shed his shirt, revealing all the wonderful planes and angles of his chest that Nasira had always appreciated. "Reptiles and fish would be more afraid of us."

"I thought you were only removing your boots."

He hung the shirt on a tree limb and swiped a palm over his nape. "It's rather warm out. Feel free to take yours off, too."

She claimed the spot on the stump Sebastian had vacated but only bared her feet. "You are so amusing."

"You are so gorgeous."

She rolled up her pants legs and stood to find the grassy earth remarkably soothing beneath her soles. "You are such a flatterer."

"I'm sincere in my compliments." He held out his hand. "Let me assist you as we explore the murky depths of an uncharted Texas *crick*."

As much as she wanted to assert her independence,

Nasira thought it best to hold on to her husband for support in the event something unknown attacked her toes. She clasped his hand and allowed him to guide her down the sloping bank and into the water. "It is much cooler than I expected," she said, her words followed by a slight shiver.

"I think it's rather nice," he replied without releasing her. "And not a sea creature in sight."

"Not any we can see. We have no idea what might be lurking beneath the surface."

"I shall protect you, fair maiden."

No sooner than he had said it, Nasira lost her footing and began to fall backward, inadvertently wrenching her hand from Sebastian's grasp. She landed on her bottom in the shallow water, sending a spray of moisture into her face.

She sputtered and wiped her eyes then looked up to find her husband standing over her. When he offered his hand, she swatted it away. "What were you saying about protecting me?"

He executed a bow. "My sincerest apologies, but you took me by surprise. You are normally very coordinated."

She came to her feet and slicked back her hair. "The bottom is as slippery as glass. And heavens, the smell."

"How can I make this up to you?"

She glared at him. "Help me out of this awful creek."

"I have a much better idea." Apparently, it included Sebastian immersing himself in the water and surfacing with a smile. "Now we are both wet and smelly."

"Lovely."

He surveyed the area a moment. "Do you know what this reminds me of?"

"I haven't a clue."

"Our trip to Tahiti."

Her mind whirled back to that grand adventure during a time when they could not get enough of each other. "If I recall, that involved a secluded cove with a waterfall, not a narrow cesspool."

"The scent isn't that foul. It's the moss."

"It has to be the cod."

"I could be mistaken, but I believe cod is a saltwater fish."

"You and your trivial facts."

When she playfully pushed at his shoulder, he swept his hand through the water and splashed her again. The battle then commenced, each trying to best the other with liquid bombs until they were both winded with laughter.

Nasira could not recall how much time had passed since they had acted with such wild abandon. How long it had been since they had shared so much laughter. She felt so connected with him, yet somewhat cautious. They still had quite a bit to resolve.

"I believe it is time to retreat," she said, but before she could evade Sebastian, he reached out and pulled her to him.

"Isn't this much better than arguing?" he asked as he guided them farther into the creek until the water lapped at her waistline.

Unable to resist her sexy, damp, shirtless husband,

she draped her arms around his neck. "I suppose it is somewhat better." And welcome. And wonderful.

He feathered a kiss across her cheek. "This is the part I remember about Tahiti."

"Only we were not fully dressed, although at least you had the foresight to remove your shirt today. I highly doubt I will ever be able to get the swampy scent out of my blouse."

"We could simply remove your blouse now."

When he reached for the buttons, she wagged a finger at him. "Now, now. We have an agreement. Conversation first."

He managed to slip open the first button and parted the placket. "What would you like to discuss?" he asked as he traced the top of her bra with a fingertip.

A topic that would ruin the mood. "Nothing at the moment. We should return to the stable with the horses since your mount seems rather restless."

He glanced at the stallion now pawing the ground. "Could I at least kiss you before we leave?"

"You usually do not ask permission."

"I'm only following the rules, per your request."

That alone should earn him a reward. "I suppose a small kiss would be all right."

Clearly her husband did not know the meaning of *small,* as if she expected him to give her anything less than a thorough kiss. Yet when he lowered his lips to hers, she found the gesture to be more tender than deep. Soft and somewhat restrained…in the beginning. And then the passion took hold. A passion she could not fight. Yet if she did not stop him now, she might not be able to stop at all.

As unwise as it seemed, at that moment she simply did not care to resist him.

Five

Before Nasira could prepare, Sebastian opened her blouse completely, unfastened her bra and lowered it enough to pay attention to her breasts. He knew precisely how to use his tongue to bring her to the point of no return. He used the pull of his mouth to great effect, causing her to tremble slightly. She clasped his head to follow his movements as he shifted from one breast to the other and closed her eyes to immerse herself in the feelings. In spite of the voice telling her to resist, she felt needy and powerless and completely under his control as he worked the clasp on her jeans, slid the zipper down and slipped his hand into her panties. And suddenly her no-sex vow went the way of the prairie wind.

Somewhere in the recesses of her mind, she knew she should tell him to stop and regain control. "Sebastian," was all she could manage in a winded voice that she barely recognized.

He raised his head and whispered in her ear, "Remember Tahiti."

She could barely remember her name in light of Sebastian's intemperate strokes between her thighs. Yet Sebastian seemed bent on teasing her into oblivion, slowing his sensual caressing as if he wanted to prolong the process. She wanted to hold off the release, and oh how she tried, but her body would no longer allow it.

In a matter of moments, she feared her legs would no longer support her as she bordered on a climax. As if her husband could sense her predicament, he tightened his grasp on her, yet he did not let up until the orgasm began to build and build. He simply told her in a low, sensual tone how she felt, what he wished to do to her. What he *would* do to her when the time was right.

Nasira stopped thinking, practically stopped breathing as she let the heady sensations take over. She rode the release wave after wave until it had subsided. And then came the regret and remorse.

"You promised me," she said as soon as she recovered her voice.

He redid her jeans and bra then buttoned her blouse. "I apologize but I could not help myself. You're very alluring when you're wet. In every sense of the word. And you have to take into account that I presently require nothing in return, therefore it's not exactly sex."

"Good grief, Sebastian, that is semantics. We were not playing tiddlywinks."

"Definitely not. No squidgers were involved."

A litany of choice words ran through her brain, yet she could only think of one ridiculous provincial phrase. "Bite me, Buck."

He had the gall to grin. "We will explore that after dinner, Beauty."

"You are…you are…such a—"

"Skilled lover?"

"Plank," she said, repeating the slang she had learned in London.

"I've been called worse than a jackass," he said as he took her by the shoulders, turned her around and patted her bottom. "Let's go, old girl, before Cappy labels us horse thieves and sends out the guard."

She trudged out of the creek, squeezed the water from the bottom of her blouse and twisted her hair into a braid. After they had donned their boots and Sebastian had put on his shirt, they mounted the horses and started back to the stable in silence.

"Are you angry with me, Sira?"

Was she? "I am not happy that I've been so weak."

"You're not weak, sweetheart. You're a woman and you have needs."

She thought back to Fiona's declaration earlier. "You are correct. I do have needs. I simply do not care for you using that as a distraction from our real problems."

"First, you're miffed because I haven't paid enough attention to you, as you pointed out so succinctly before you left London. Now that I am attempting to make up for lost time, you no longer want my consideration. Which is it, Sira? Hands on or hands off?"

She wanted to scream from frustration. "Ignoring me isn't only about withholding lovemaking, Sebastian."

"Forgive me for facilitating your orgasm. All three of them, if my memory serves me correctly. Should you require another, you'll have to ask."

Nasira glanced at Sebastian to see if he appeared as angry as he sounded. "I will not be asking until I am assured we are on the right path to mending our marriage."

"That is your call."

Without warning, Sebastian took off again and this time, she immediately followed. Yet the gelding was not as fast as the stallion and her husband arrived a few paces ahead of her. After Sebastian dismounted and headed into the barn, she soon followed suit and led the Gus inside.

When Sebastian did not afford her a glance, Nasira tied the gelding to the stall's railing and faced him. "I know you are upset with me, but—"

"Upset?" He loosened the girth strap, pulled the saddled off and turned toward her. "Why would I be upset when my wife seems bent on rejecting my attempts to recapture some intimacy?"

She bristled at his hypocrisy. "Now you understand how I have felt the past six months."

He set the saddle on the nearby stand a bit harder than necessary. "I see. Your actions and words are based on retribution."

Something about his observation rang true. "As I have said several times, I refuse to have my libido cloud my judgment."

He released a cynical laugh. "I do not recall any refusal when I had my hand down your pants earlier."

The comment brought about a searing heat between her thighs, causing her to shift from one leg to the other. Before she could retort, Cappy came down the stairs and when he reached the aisle, gave them both a long once-over. "Did you two not understand the nekkid swimming part?"

The heat shifted to Nasira's face. "Actually, we were wading in the water and I slipped."

"I had to rescue her from the creek's clutches," Sebastian added. "My wife can be quite clumsy at times."

Cappy sported a skeptical look as he loosened the girth strap on Gus's saddle. "In case you're hungry, the missus put a roast in the oven for the two of you. She said it should be ready in about an hour and she'll be back later to clean up."

"I can do the dishes," Nasira began, "although I would like to meet her and tell her thank you."

"Annie's a stickler for giving people their privacy, and I'm thinkin' that's exactly what you two need, so I'll tell her you'll handle the cleanup."

Nasira didn't want the man getting the wrong idea. "We truly do not require privacy, Cappy. She is welcome anytime."

"If you say so." He pulled the saddle off Gus's back and grinned. "By the way, ma'am, you missed a couple of buttons."

Too mortified to offer an explanation, Nasira turned to retreat to the house without looking back, the sound of the men's laughter following her for the next few meters.

She was so angry, she practically stomped up the path. If her husband thought he would escape her ire, he was sorely mistaken. As soon as she took a shower, she planned to confront Sebastian over his amusement at her expense. Until that point, she would simply avoid him.

"Sira, wait up."

Nasira quickened her gait in response to the directive. "I am not speaking to you."

"Actually, darling, you just did."

Infuriating man. "Go away, Sebastian."

"Not until you give me the opportunity to apologize."

"I am not in a benevolent mood."

The comment seemed to encourage Sebastian's silence, or that was what she thought until she heard, "Damn my leg."

Only then did she turn around to discover her husband bent at the waist, both palms resting on his thighs. She could leave him standing on the path in pain, or she could see about his injury.

Nasira turned around, strode to him and hovered above him. "Did you suffer a wound?"

"Only to my pride."

Then he raised his gaze to her, grinned, grabbed her around the waist and tossed her over his shoulder caveman-style. "Let me down, you brute!" she said, to no avail.

"Not until we arrive at our destination."

"I cannot believe you lied to me about your leg."

"Actually, I did have a slight twitch of momentary pain."

"I have trouble believing that. Granted, you will have several pains if you continue to carry me like a bag of grain."

"Sira, you are many things. Weighty is not one of them."

She supposed she should consider that a compliment.

Once they reached the deck, Sebastian climbed the stairs and put Nasira down, yet kept her hand clasped in his. "I beg your forgiveness for my inconsiderate laughter in the stable. However, I did defend your honor after your departure."

She folded her arms around her middle. "Was that before or after you morphed into a Neanderthal?"

"I believe that was after I beat my chest and declared you my woman."

"You are such a comedian, Sebastian."

"I am a man quite enamored of his gorgeous wife, and I do hope she will forgive me."

She wanted so badly to remain angry at him, but he possessed the power of persuasion usually reserved for practiced barristers. "You are forgiven. Can I please bathe now?"

He winked. "Do you require assistance?"

"No, I do not."

Without awaiting a reply, Nasira turned and entered the house to wash away the remnants of murky river water—and the mistake she had made by believing she could distance herself from her husband, physically and emotionally. The more she was with him, the more she realized how good the majority of their marriage had been. Worse still, she recognized how much she truly loved him.

And as she walked into the bedroom and spotted the bracelet on the bureau, the reminder of their loss, she questioned whether he would be willing to give her the one thing she wanted most from him.

Only time would tell.

Sebastian sat alone at the dining room table, staring at the familiar number splashed across his cell phone screen. He needed to answer the call but dreaded it all the same.

After one more ring, Sebastian swiped the screen and said, "Hello, Stella."

"For pity's sake, Sebastian, where are you?"

His stepmother was nothing if not direct. "Texas."

"You went after her even after I advised against it."

"Yes, but before you go off on the virtue of patience, she is my wife and I have every right to seek her out."

"Yes, you do, yet it could make matters much worse."

"We're getting along famously."

"I hope that is the case," she said skeptically.

"It is. How is Father?"

The slight hesitation had him bracing for bad news. "Actually, he's had a cheery day. He played chess with the butler this morning."

Odd that his patriarch could remember how to play a board game yet at times forgot his own son's name. "That's good. He's a tough old guy."

"Yes, but might I remind you, the last time you spoke

to the physician, he told you he's going to continue to fade away, little by little, until we won't recognize the man he used to be, and he quite possibly will not recognize us."

Sebastian didn't need to be reminded of that. "I know, Stella. That's why it's imperative I work out my problems with Nasira and return to London as soon as feasible."

"And that is why you must consider having a child as soon as possible. I would like your father to go to the hereafter knowing he has an heir."

As if Sebastian needed more pressure in the procreation department. After all, his father had been partially responsible for his reluctance to try again with Nasira and wholly responsible for Sebastian's mother's death. "There is no guarantee that will happen before his demise."

"The doctor believes he still has a few years left in him."

But would they be good years?

Sebastian looked up to see Nasira standing in the open doorway, giving him a good excuse to cut the conversation short. "I will take your request under advisement. In the meantime, I'm going to have dinner with my wife. Tell Father hello from both of us."

Stella barely had time to say goodbye before Sebastian ended the call. He pushed the phone aside and studied Nasira. Her long, silky black hair cascaded over her shoulders. She wore a pink sleeveless blouse that complemented her golden skin and white loose-fitting slacks that hid her best attributes. Not an issue. He knew exactly what the cotton fabric concealed.

"You look very pretty tonight."

She pulled back the chair across from him and sat. "Thank you. I see you've gone from cowboy to corporate billionaire. If I had known you were going to wear a suit and tie I would have donned an evening gown."

"Force of habit," he said as he shrugged out of his jacket and laid it on the seat next to him. "Better?"

"A bit more casual." She bent her elbow on the table and supported her cheek with her palm. "Did you do all this?"

"Will I score a few points if I said yes?"

"You will score points if you tell me the truth."

"Actually, the table was already set. I did remove the food from the oven."

"It smells wonderful," she said as she unfolded the white napkin and laid it in her lap, prompting Sebastian to follow suit.

"That it does."

When he reached for her plate, she waved him away. "I am quite capable of helping myself."

"Far be it for me to tread on your independence."

She took a less-than-generous helping of the roast beef and vegetables. "You have a habit of doing that."

"I do?"

"Yes, you do. I suppose I cannot fault you considering I was rather helpless when we married."

She had been the picture of innocence. "You've grown quite a bit, Sira."

"I would hope so after ten years." She took a bite

then a drink of water from the cut-crystal glass. "Evidently Annie is fond of salt."

Sebastian took a much bigger bite of the fare and found it to his liking. But he thought it best to be as agreeable as possible. "Perhaps a bit. I just spoke with Stella. She told me to give you her regards."

"How is James?"

"She said he had a good day, right after she lectured me on leaving without giving her notice."

Nasira's brown eyes widened. "You didn't tell her you were coming here?"

"I left word through the servants. It was very much a spontaneous decision."

"I am certain she was worried."

"Possibly, but she was more concerned about other issues."

"What issues?"

He was hoping she wouldn't ask. "You know Stella. She is a broken record when it comes to producing an heir."

"That is understandable, Sebastian. She knows how badly your father would like to see that happen."

He had suddenly lost his appetite. "My father has no right to dictate my future after what he did..." He refused to go there for if he did, he would have to offer an explanation.

"What did he do, Sebastian?"

He took another bite that now tasted bitter as brine. "I'd prefer not to discuss it."

Nasira wadded the napkin and tossed it on the table.

"This is exactly the reason we are having problems. Your inability to communicate drives me batty."

"It's complicated, Sira. I see no point in dredging up the past."

"Perhaps you should since it's apparently affecting our future."

He shoved back from the table and began to pace. "You are asking too much of me."

"I am only asking for honesty, Sebastian. My intent is not to cause you pain. Does this have something to do with your mother?"

He turned midstride and faced her. "It has everything do with her."

"Please, come sit and tell me about her. Surely you have good memories."

More than she would ever know, unless he finally told her. Then he could gradually move into the bad, if he dared.

He reclaimed his seat and stared at the food now growing cold on his plate. "I have no idea how to begin to tell you about Martha Ella Edwards."

Nasira set her plate aside and folded her arms atop the table. "I know you were ten when she passed, so I suppose you can begin by telling me what you do remember."

He smiled at the recollections, the special moments that he had never shared. The painful times he couldn't share, at least not now. "She was extremely devoted to my father and to me. She used to call me her little drummer boy because I had a penchant for stealing wooden spoons from the kitchen and banging them on anything stationary."

"Clearly you were destined to be in a rock band."

"I thought that too after Mother bought me a real set of drums on my eighth birthday. But of course James could not endure the noise and had the servants toss them two days later."

Nasira laid her palm on his hand, which was now resting on the tabletop. "I am so sorry, Sebastian. I know you and your father have always seemed to be at odds, but I assumed that had to do with the two of you butting horns over business like two battering rams."

If she only knew the reason behind Sebastian's well-hidden resentment. If he let down his guard, she would. "I never approved of the way he treated my mother, as if she were no more than a concubine put on this earth for his pleasure."

"How could you believe that at such a young age? Was he inappropriate in your presence?"

"No. I only learned some facts later and drew my own conclusions."

"You are going to have to be less vague in order for me to help you move past this."

"I don't need your help, Sira, or your pity."

"I would never pity you, Sebastian, but I do believe you need to have someone as a sounding board. And I would hope after ten years together you could trust me enough to fill that role."

He pondered her words a moment and realized she was probably right. He also knew that by being totally transparent, he would be inviting a measure of pain. Yet he couldn't think of one soul he trusted more than his wife, and he had done her a disservice by not revealing his secrets. Only after doing so would she understand why he could not in good conscience go forward with their plans to have a child.

"I will tell you what you believe you want to know, but I assure you it's not pretty."

"I am stronger than you think, Sebastian."

He would not debate that. At times he wondered if she possessed more strength than him. "This secret, the one no one speaks of, has to do with my mother's demise."

Nasira leaned forward and sent him a concerned look. "Please tell me and end this suspense."

He drew in a deep breath and prepared to lower the boom. "My father killed her."

Six

Nasira placed a hand over her mouth to stifle a gasp. Myriad questions whirled through her mind like a crazed carousel. "Why? How?"

Sebastian disappeared into the kitchen and returned with a tumbler half full of his favorite scotch. "Why? Because he's a selfish bastard who only cares about his desires. *How* involves… "

When he hesitated, Nasira's anxiety escalated. "Go on."

Sebastian streaked a hand over his shadowed jaw. "He knew she was ill and didn't lift a finger to help her."

She sat back, her shoulders sagging from mild relief. "I truly thought you were going to mention knives or guns or perhaps poison."

He settled back into the chair and took a sip of the

drink. "He might as well have put a gun to her head by not seeking medical attention when she clearly needed it. I knew something was wrong that morning."

Nasira realized he was perched on the precipice of deep emotional pain. "The morning she passed away?"

He shook his head. "No. The last morning I saw her alive." He stared at some unknown focal point, as if he had mentally returned to that day, before he spoke again. "I had been on summer break from boarding school and it was time for me to return. Of course, I happened to be running late when Mother summoned me into her quarters. She was propped up in bed and she looked very pale. She told me she loved me and hugged me as if she didn't want to let me go. As if she knew it would be the final time. And I wrenched out of her grasp because I knew if I didn't leave at that moment, I would earn my father's wrath for making the driver wait. I never expressed my love for her, and I have lived with that regret for almost three decades."

Her heart ached for him. "You were only a child, Sebastian. You could not have foreseen the future."

He released a weary sigh. "Perhaps, and I would not have predicted what I would learn when I was called into the headmaster's office two days later. My father did not bother to personally retrieve me. He sent one of the bloody staff members to tell me my mother was dead. He did not shed one tear at the wake. Worse still, he admonished me for crying."

Nasira had always been fond of her father-in-law, who seemed nothing at all like the tyrant Sebastian had described. "I am stunned at his behavior. James has always treated me with kindness and affection."

Sebastian leveled his gaze on her. "You've never disappointed him, and I have never lived up to his standards."

"You are a brilliant businessman. I cannot imagine he would hand over the company to you if he did not truly believe that."

"He did so because he had no choice since I failed to produce an heir. I refuse to relinquish that control to him."

Had this been the reason behind his reluctance to have another child? A vendetta against an unfeeling patriarch?

She would not know the reason behind his resistance unless she asked, yet she sensed this might not be the time or place to do so. She did have another important question. "I understand James treated you poorly, but do you truly believe he neglected your mother's health issues? I've heard the staff speaking highly of their relationship."

Sebastian tightened his grip on the glass in his hand. "I heard the servants discussing a few details when they didn't realize I was eavesdropping. As we both know, they are the eyes and ears of the household."

"And did you confront your father over this idle chit-chat?"

He pushed the scotch aside as if it held no appeal. "At ten years old, I didn't dare try. Since that time, he has never been one to discuss personal affairs. Had I inquired, he would have dismissed me, as he did whenever I asked anything about my mother."

Her husband had based his conclusions on rumors, not fact, and that bothered Nasira. "Have you considered talking to Stella to verify what you heard all those years ago?"

"Yes, and she stated she wasn't at liberty to provide the details. Then she advised me to stop living in the past."

Stella's reluctance to clear the air was unacceptable as far as Nasira was concerned, albeit an indication of her devotion to James. But she did not feel she had the right to intervene…yet. Right now, she was thankful Sebastian had begun to open up for the first time during their union. She did not want to push her luck by applying too much pressure. "I am really very sorry about what you've endured, Sebastian. I wish there was more I could do or say to ease your distress."

"I'm not distressed," he said as he pushed back from the table and stood. "But there is something you could do."

She could only imagine what he had in mind. "Yes?"

"Accompany me to the festival downtown."

The request totally took her by surprise. "What festival?"

"I'm not certain. I believe it involves street vendors and a carnival. I thought it might be a good way to soak in the culture."

Quite possibly a good way to temporarily erase the past, Nasira thought. Understandable he would want to do that, and this time she would allow it. Still, she certainly would not refuse the opportunity to spend some quality time with her husband. She came to her feet and attempted a smile. "That sounds wonderful. I suppose I should change."

He stood, rounded the table and then touched her face. "You're a beautiful, remarkable woman, Sira. Never think you should change for me."

The sheer emotion in his eyes, the absolute sincerity in his voice, sent Nasira's spirits soaring. Perhaps they had reached a turning point, the prospect of a new beginning. Yet she acknowledged they would not obtain that goal until her husband was willing to tell her the unabridged truth.

Sebastian had avoided the whole truth like a practiced coward. He hadn't told his wife that rejecting parenthood had more to do with his fear for her safety and not his determination to avoid his father's interference. Someday he would reveal the bitter details behind his mother's death, but right now he wanted to leave the past behind and concentrate on the present.

With that in mind, he took Nasira's hand into his as they strolled the streets of Royal crowded with cowboys and kids, two of whom sprinted past them on the sidewalk.

"This place is certainly full of children," he said. "I'd expect to see the Pied Piper coming around the corner at any moment."

Nasira sent him a frown. "This is a festival, Sebastian. What else would you expect?"

Better manners. "True. The town appears to treat

procreation as a sport as revered as their Friday night Texas football."

As they continued on, one particular display caught his curiosity and caused him to pause. "What in the bloody hell is cow patty bingo?"

Nasira's gaze traveled to the group gathered around the exhibition. "Well, it clearly involves a cow and some sort of game board and... I believe it is best we keep walking."

He couldn't contain his laughter. "I could not agree more."

They continued on past several artisans with tables full of their wares. As they approached one fresh-faced young woman with baskets of multicolored flowers, Sebastian halted, released his wife's hand and selected a single red rose. "How much is this?"

"Two dollars," the blonde replied. "Or six for ten dollars."

"One will do." He withdrew his wallet from his rear pocket and pulled out a twenty-dollar bill. "Here you go. Keep the proceeds."

The teen appeared awestruck. "Thanks bunches. It's for a good cause."

"What cause would that be?"

"A new football stadium."

He started to argue that an orphanage would constitute a better cause, but thought better of it. "Best of luck on your venture," he said, then turned to Nasira. "For my lovely bride."

She took the rose and smiled as if he had offered the

moon and stars, not a simple posy. "To what do I owe this wonderful gift?"

He kissed her cheek. "For agreeing to wed the likes of me."

"Most of the time, I happen to like being wed to the likes of you."

She might rescind her half compliment if she knew of the lies he still harbored. "Shall we take our chances on the games up ahead?"

"As long as they do not involve cow patties."

"I believe they are games of skill involving tossing rings."

She hooked her arm through his. "Then by all means, let us test your skills."

Unable to help himself, Sebastian leaned over and whispered, "I'm definitely up for testing all my skills when we return to the ranch."

He expected his spouse to deliver a derisive glare over the innuendo. Instead, he received a surprisingly sultry look. "That is altogether possible if you are a good boy tonight."

Perhaps Rafe had been correct—simple gestures could pay off in spades.

When they traveled on toward the brightly-lit gaming booths, Sebastian spotted a young boy dressed in jeans and miniature cowboy boots, turning in circles in the middle of the sidewalk, swiping the tears furiously from his face. A group of boisterous teens approached him, seemingly oblivious to the distressed child.

Sensing disaster, Sebastian immediately removed Nasira's hand from his arm, swept the boy up and away from the danger of getting run over by unconcerned adolescents, then set him down near a street light, away from the crowd. "Are you lost, young man?"

He turned his misty brown eyes on him and sniffed. "My dad told me not to talk to strangers."

Sebastian took a step back so the boy wouldn't feel threatened. "That is banner advice under normal circumstances. I only want to help you locate your parents and return you safely to them."

The child seemed to mull that over a minute before he spoke again. "A girl was chasing me and I lost my dad."

"What does your father look like?" Nasira asked from behind Sebastian.

When the boy turned his gaze on Nasira, he seemed to relax and smiled as if he were quite smitten. "He's got on a cowboy hat and boots and jeans and I think a blue shirt. Where'd you get it?" he asked, looking at the rose.

"Sebastian gave it to me." She pointed behind her. "We bought it at a booth not far from here."

"I might want to get one of those for my…" He lowered his eyes and kicked a pebble into the street. "Mom."

After exchanging a knowing look with Sebastian, Nasira offered him the flower. "I am certain my husband would not mind if you give her this one."

"Not at all." He did mind that the description of the missing parent didn't provide much hope of immediately finding him. "Is your father tall like me?"

He nodded. "Uh huh. But he doesn't talk funny like you. Are you from Dallas?"

Nasira laughed. "We are from London, far across the ocean."

The child's expression brightened. "We learned about that place in school. I'm in the second grade and I like to ride horses and... Dad!"

Clutching the rose, the boy ran straight into the arms of a man sporting a suspicious look as he headed toward them. As soon as he arrived, Sebastian thought it best to offer an explanation before the presumed father jumped to the wrong conclusion. "We found your son quite distressed and lost. It seems you've arrived just in the nick of time."

"Looks that way," the cowboy said as he eyed the flower before regarding his child. "You know better than to run off without me, Brady. Your mother's going to skin my hide for not watching you better."

"I didn't mean to do it," Brady said. "Angie was chasing me and I ran too far, I guess. And then this man picked me up before I got run over by kids and the lady gave me her flower so I could give it to Mom."

"Mom, huh?" the father asked.

Brady shrugged and muttered, "Maybe Angie," then turned his attention back to Nasira and Sebastian. "They're from London. Do you know about London, Dad?"

"Yep, I do," he replied. "I also know that I told you to stay away from people you don't know."

Sebastian offered his hand for a shake in an effort to reassure the man. "I'm Sebastian Edwards."

The cowboy hesitantly accepted the gesture. "I'm Gavin McNeal, former sheriff."

No wonder he had looked at Sebastian as if he were a deviant. "You're no longer in law enforcement?"

His features went from rock hard to only slightly stony. "I gave that up to spend more time with this kiddo, and the one we have on the way. I'm a full-time rancher now, although I do pull deputy duty now and again if the department's shorthanded."

A clear message to Sebastian the cowboy could still hold his own around unwelcome strangers. "I'm certain your service to the community is very much appreciated. And to put your mind at ease, Brady did mention he wasn't allowed to talk to strangers. Of course, I assure you our intentions were perfectly honorable."

"Yes, they were." Nasira moved to Sebastian's side. "However, my husband has forgotten his manners as he has failed to introduce me."

That could be a rather large strike against him. "My apologies. This is my wife, Nasira."

"I am Rafiq bin Saleed's sister," Nasira added. "You might know him."

"Only by reputation," Gavin said. "I did hear something about some folks from England staying at the Shakirs' place, so I assume that's you. My ranch isn't too far from there and my wife, Valerie, and Fiona are fairly good friends."

Apparently news traveled at warp speed in this dusty Texas town. "We're only going to be here for a few weeks. Do you have any suggestions on sights we should see while we're here?"

"You should have dinner at the Texas Cattleman's Club," he said. "And when you do, be sure to check out the statue of Jessamine Golden. That's my wife's great-great-grandmother."

"I have seen the statue," Nasira said. "But I am sure my husband will find it quite interesting."

Brady began tugging on his father's hand to garner his attention. "Can we go ride the roller coaster now?"

"Sure thing, bud, as soon as I find your mama, who was hanging out near the arts and crafts last time I looked." Gavin regarded them again. "Nice to meet you folks, and thanks for corralling the kid. What do you say to Mr. and Mrs. Edwards, Brady?"

"Thank you for getting me not lost and for giving me the flower."

"You are quite welcome," Sebastian said.

"Goodbye, Brady," Nasira added. "I hope you have a wonderful time this evening, and I am certain Angie will appreciate the rose."

Gavin took Brady's hand and touched the brim of his hat. "Have a good night, folks."

Watching father and son walked away, Sebastian experienced a good deal of regret as he remembered a time in the distant past when he'd had the same relationship with his own father. The relationship that at one time he'd hoped to have with his own son, until he realized the lack of wisdom in that. He was amused as Brady started chattering about the funny-talking man being a superhero, and did they have those in London?

The comment caused Sebastian to chuckle. "From shipping magnate to superhero. Quite a leap."

Nasira tucked her arm into his again as they started

down the sidewalk. "I would thoroughly disagree. You are a natural-born rescuer."

He frowned. "I wouldn't go that far."

She tipped her head against his shoulder. "I would. In a sense you rescued me."

He had never looked at his marriage offer in that way, but he understood why she might. "Perhaps I saved you from a life of misery with a forced marriage to a man chosen for you, but you would have found a way out of the predicament without my assistance."

"I suppose that is possible," she said. "But I am glad that I met you that night at the gala."

"I'm grateful you gave me a second glance considering all those potential suitors surrounding you."

"Yes, but not one offered to whisk me away in their Bentley."

They exchanged a smile and walked on in silence, but one question nagged at Sebastian. "Have you enjoyed our life together, Sira?"

She paused a moment before answering. "We have had wonderful adventures and amazing travel. You have introduced me to many new experiences."

"No regrets?"

"Only one."

"What would that be?" he asked though he already knew the answer.

"We have no children."

He had strolled right into that one. "I understand you're still mourning the loss, yet I can't understand why you would want to risk your health after you had such a difficult pregnancy."

She stopped and faced him. "Life is not without risk, Sebastian. And at times risk comes with precious rewards."

He didn't know how to answer to satisfy her needs. He didn't know if he would ever want to enter that territory again. "Speaking of risks, would you care to climb on that giant Ferris wheel and take it for a spin?"

Nasira glanced over her shoulder then regarded him with a frown. "You know I am afraid of heights."

"You have no need to be afraid while in the presence of a superhero."

She smiled. "This is true. If I agree, will you promise to hold on to me?"

"You may count on my undivided attention."

"Then yes, I will join you on that contraption, and hope I do live long enough to regret it."

Sebastian led Nasira to the line of people awaiting their turn on the ride. When their time came, he approached the elderly gentleman in charge of the ride and withdrew his wallet. "How much, kind sir?"

"Three tickets."

Tickets? "I wasn't aware we needed those." He pulled a twenty out of his pocket. "Will this do?"

"I don't make change, mister."

"No change necessary."

The attendant grinned, displaying a remarkable lack of teeth. "I guess it'll do at that."

"Amazing how money opens doors," Sebastian said as they climbed into the car.

Nasira grabbed the railing and sat, looking somewhat fearful. "Amazing how rickety this ride seems."

He lowered next to her and wrapped his arm around her shoulder. "Just hold tight to your knight."

She surprised him with a soft kiss. "Happily, kind sir."

When the wheel began to move, sending them up toward the night sky, Nasira closed her eyes and tensed against him. He held her tighter, stroked her arm and rested his lips against her temple. He experienced such a fierce need to keep her sheltered from harm, and a secret fear that he could not be the man she would want in the future if he couldn't give her the child she desired.

But tonight, he could give her all his consideration and forget the chasm that still existed between them.

When they reached the top, the ride jolted to a stop, causing the car to slightly sway and his wife to clutch his thigh in a death grip. Stifling a wince, Sebastian lifted her hand and kissed her palm. "Open your eyes, sweetheart."

"Must I?"

"No, but you're missing an extraordinary view."

After a few seconds ticked off, she finally lifted her lids and looked around. "I must admit, all the lights are beautiful. They remind me of our holiday together two years ago."

While she must have been struck by sentimentality, he was hit by some rather sexual memories. "Ah, yes. Rome. We barely left the room."

"That is not true. We had several meals on the veranda."

He brushed a kiss across her lips. "That's not all we did on that veranda."

Her smile arrived slowly. "True. You have always been quite devilish when we travel."

"And you are always quite willing to dance with the devil."

"Evidently I cannot resist your charms."

He pushed her hair away from her shoulder. "Would you be willing to dance with me later tonight?"

Without giving him a verbal response, Nasira wrapped her hand around his nape and pulled his mouth to hers, taking Sebastian by surprise. As the ride began to move again, picking up speed, they continued to kiss as if they were youngsters in the throes of first love. But they weren't youngsters. They were husband and wife in the midst of a troubled marriage, yet he felt as if this could be the path to healing.

When the ride bumped to a stop, they finally ended the kiss only to be met by applause, whistles and cat-calls. Sebastian helped Nasira out of the car and they rushed away, then paused and shared in a few laughs.

Nasira wrapped her arms around his waist. "I do believe you have ruined my reputation."

He pressed a kiss on her forehead. "If you agree to return to the ranch now, I will endeavor to ruin it more."

She studied his eyes for a few moments, as if searching for something unknown there. "Sebastian, I...."

"What, sweetheart?"

"I think that is a marvelous idea."

Saying what she had wanted to say would have been a horrible idea.

Still, Nasira had come very close to voicing an emotion she had never admitted to him, or to herself, during their decade together. She loved him, and most likely had for many years. Love had not been a goal in their marriage. A marriage based on convenience and mutual need. Yet somehow she had introduced the emotion into the union when she had allowed Sebastian into her life, and into her heart.

That did not change the fact that her husband might not feel more than fondness for her. That did not negate that they wanted to journey down different paths and if he had his way, their future would not include having a child.

Yet as she rode back to the ranch, her hand resting lightly in Sebastian's, she did not care about compromise or doubts. She only wanted to enjoy this night with her husband in the event these memorable moments might be their last.

She leaned back against the headrest and sighed. "I realized something tonight that I have never considered before."

"You are not so afraid of heights?"

"No. I enjoy country living."

"That's why we have the country home in Bath to escape the hectic pace in London proper."

"I know, yet I feel a certain freedom here. It does sound odd, I suppose."

He pulled beneath the portico and shut off the ignition. "This place does afford quite a bit of privacy, which reminds me." He reached into the back of the car, retrieved a silver bag full of pink tissue and handed it to her.

"What is this?"

"Open it and you'll see."

She rummaged around and withdrew a bathing suit that was little more than a labyrinth of turquoise strings. "I have never flown a kite in the dark."

"Very amusing. We both need to relax, and what better way to do that than to swim."

"Isn't it too cool to swim?"

"The spa and pool are both heated."

She could imagine they would generate their own heat, yet she worried about the privacy issue. "I would still have to get out of the spa or pool." She shook the swimsuit at him. "This barely covers anything at all. What if someone happens upon us?"

"You have a robe, do you not?"

"Yes."

"Besides, you have a remarkable body. Why not show it off?"

"I do not think it is wise to show off my body this much when two other people reside on the property."

"Two people who've been instructed to give us complete solitude."

He had supported his arguments much too well, drat him. "All right. I will join you in a swim." She pointed at him. "But only for a swim. Heaven knows I wouldn't want to be caught doing anything else."

He gave her a winning grin, the one that had always won her over. Patently sensual, and slightly wicked. "Yes, dear. Only a swim."

As much as she would like to trust him, Nasira was not sure she should. Trouble was, could she trust herself?

Seven

The moment Nasira stepped onto the deck and slipped off the robe, swimming was the last thing on Sebastian's mind. The suit fit her to perfection, from the low cut of the bodice to the bottoms secured by two ribbons at her rounded hips that accentuated her long torso. Her hair flowed freely, straight and sleek, begging for his touch. When he honed in on the diamond hoop at her navel, her attempt at rebellion during her brief university days, he had fond memories of playing with the bauble with his tongue…as well as other more intimate places now covered by a small fabric triangle. That alone caused him to move down one stair to conceal the result of his sinful thoughts.

He had to remember to take it slowly, let the evening progress with no expectations in terms of lovemaking.

He needed to concentrate on making his wife feel appreciated and respected, even if it meant using his tongue solely to talk for the time being.

Unfortunately his randy libido seemed to be speaking much louder than his honor. He would simply have to quiet the urges and not appear as impatient as a lustful schoolboy.

Down, Henry.

When Nasira stuck her toe in the deep end of the pool to test the water, even that seemed overtly sexy to Sebastian. And when she executed a perfect dive, surfaced not far from him and slicked her hair back from her gorgeous face, he gritted his teeth to keep from going after her like a lion and a gazelle.

"Bravo," he said as she waded toward him. "You're a regular little mermaid."

She lifted her hair to secure the tie at her neck. "I almost had equipment failure when I dove in. Could you have not found something a bit more modest?"

At the moment he realized that might have worked better in light of his burgeoning erection. But then again, probably not. She could be wearing a heavy trench coat and he would still want her, especially if she were nude beneath it. He would like very much for her to be nude beneath him. Or perhaps on top of him. Standing up against the deck would also work to his satisfaction...

"Have you been rendered mute, Sebastian?"

For the most part, yes. "I'm sorry. Did you ask me something?"

"Never mind." She joined him on the step, keeping

a relatively safe distance between them. "The house-keeper turned down my bed. Did you notice if she is still here?"

No, but he did notice that if the bikini were a bit lower, he could possibly see her nipples. "I'm almost certain she performed those tasks while we were away."

Sira leaned forward, causing the top to gape and allowing him the view again. "It would probably behoove us to check."

"That might be breast." *Dammit*. "I mean *best*."

She sent him a mock scolding look. "I have barely been in here five minutes and you are already misbehaving."

Guilty. "It was only a verbal faux pas, Sira."

"Then take care to mind your mouth."

And he did…by planting it on her mouth, disregarding his earlier cautions about going slowly. He expected she might shove him away, or perhaps push him into the water, yet she joined in as if she needed this as badly as he did.

After they parted, she tipped her head against his forehead. "I hate that I am so helpless around you."

He lifted her chin and forced her to look at him. "You are not helpless in the least, and you are not an innocent. You are as drawn to the devil in me as I am the vixen in you."

"So you think."

"So I know."

He loosened the ties at her neck but paused before he went further. "Tell me you do not want me and I'll stop."

"I…cannot."

Which was all the encouragement Sebastian needed to continue. He removed her top, tossed it aside and then toyed with the band riding low on her hips. "Stop now?"

She released a ragged sigh. "No."

After he slid her bottoms away and draped them on the chrome railing, he led her into waist-deep water and kissed her, his hands roving over her breasts. She soon pulled away, moved back and smiled. "The vixen says take off your bathing suit."

"Far be it for me to argue with her," he said as he shoved down his trunks, stepped out of them with effort, and hurled them onto the deck.

She crooked her finger at him. "Come here, devil."

They came together in another blast of heat, of that passion they'd known from the beginning. She scraped her nails down his back, while he attacked her neck with kisses and brought her legs up around his waist. It would be so easy to take her here, take her now, yet the nagging concerns over pregnancy prevented him from doing so. He should have brought the blasted condoms with him.

"Do it," she whispered with desperation as she reached beneath the water, took his erection in hand, and guided it inside her.

Driven by pure lust and need, he thrust into her, twice, before he gathered every ounce of strength and pulled out. "The bedroom," he managed around his labored respiration.

She looked at him and blinked twice. "Why?"

"More privacy." A lame excuse but the only one he could provide without completely destroying the mood.

"All right," she said as she lowered to her feet. "But hurry."

That request he could categorically fulfill, and he did as he took her by the hand and led her to the chaise on the pool deck. They wrapped up in the towels he'd brought, periodically kissing and intimately touching as they headed into the house. Once they reached the corridor leading to the guest suite, he paused and backed her against the wall immediately outside the door to his quarters.

He wanted her to remember this, to know how badly he wanted her, to make her want him as much. He parted the towel and suckled her breasts, first one, then the other, before sliding his lips down her torso.

Then he went to his knees, nudged her legs apart and sent his mouth on a mission between her thighs. He used his tongue to divide her warm flesh, tracing circles around and around that intimate spot, intent on driving her wild.

She bowed over him, running her hands over his scalp, her breaths coming in short pants. She dug her nails into his back so deeply, he thought she might have drawn blood. He didn't care. Giving her pleasure was well worth the pain.

"Sebastian." His name came out of her mouth in a harsh whisper as he stroked her with his tongue softly, then harder as he covered her completely with his mouth and suckled that sweet spot.

Her legs began to tremble and a low, sexual sound filtered out of her as she began to orgasm. He didn't let up until he had ridden out every pulse of the climax, then he kissed his way back up her beautiful body.

She reached for him again and demanded, "Now."

"Not yet," he said as he clasped her wrist to still her hand. Otherwise the act would be over in short order.

Without protesting, Nasira followed him into his bedroom. While she turned down the comforter, he opened the nightstand drawer and retrieved the silver packets. He turned and found her stretched out on her back on the bed, her damp hair a sexy, tangled mess, her knees bent in preparation for him. Yet when she spied the condoms in his grasp, she suddenly sat up on the edge of the mattress and lowered her eyes.

After laying the packets on the side table, he claimed the space beside her and rested a hand on her bare leg. "I realize this isn't what you want, but under the circumstance, it's a necessity."

Her gaze snapped to his, the haze of desire completely gone. "Is it?"

"We still have much to discuss in regard to that issue, by your own admission."

She pushed her hair back from her face. "Yes, you're right, but the reminder of our impasse took me aback for a moment. I suppose I simply wanted to forget our dilemma this evening. I wish you could have held off with the condoms a bit longer."

Frustration brought him to his feet to face her. "This wouldn't have been a bloody issue if you'd started taking the pill again."

"As I've said, I had no reason to do that when you were so bent on ignoring me." She pinched the bridge of her nose and momentarily closed her eyes. "I am so angry."

"At me?"

"At myself. I have walked into the same trap, succumbing to your charisma and allowing you to lead me away from our problems."

Now he was angry. "I did nothing of the sort. We are husband and wife and we should thank our lucky stars we still want each other so fiercely after ten years of marriage."

She let loose with a cynical laugh. "Of course you would see it that way. But sex is not a cure-all for serious marital problems."

If she only realized that was the only way he knew how to communicate his true feelings for her. The right words had never come easily for him. Neither had acknowledging his emotions. "Why can you not be happy with what we have? Why do you see the need to change everything?"

She pulled the sheet up to cover herself. "Because we cannot be truly happy unless we fix what is broken. Only until you open up to me completely can we move past our problems."

He knew where she was going, and he didn't want to bloody go there. "I've told you more about my mother's death than I've ever told another soul."

"Yet you have not told me everything, Sebastian. Aside from your father's careless disregard and your guilt over your last moments with your mother, there is something else keeping you from committing to fatherhood."

He clenched his jaw against the litany of curses threatening to spill out. "You have no idea what I went through."

She stood and leveled her gaze on him. "Then tell me all of it. Make me understand."

He didn't dare. "I am going to take a shower."

He turned to retire to the bath, only to have her call him back. "When will you stop running away, Sebastian?" she asked. "When it is too late for us?"

The words impaled him like a knife to his heart. "You're asking too much of me tonight, Sira. If it's too difficult for you to be intimate with me, then by all means, retire to your blessed bed and I'll stay in mine alone. If you happen to change your mind, then it will be up to you to come to me. In the meantime, I'll not bother you again."

And this time, he vowed to stay true to his word.

He had not spoken to her for two days. In fact, Nasira had barely seen her husband except in passing. He had spent much of his time in his quarters, sequestered away with his laptop.

Today that would come to an end, if she had any say in the matter. She had given him a wide berth to think about what she had said, but they had come to a crossroads. His time was up.

She opened the door to his bedroom without knocking, only to find him packing. A blinding fear overcame her, then resignation that perhaps she had pushed him too hard.

He afforded her only a glance while he placed a suit in the garment bag without speaking.

"Are you returning to London?" she asked, expecting an affirmative answer.

"No. I'm going to Dallas," he said, shattering her expectations, and filling her with relief.

She moved closer to the bed, but not too close. "Why Dallas?"

He dropped a few toiletries into a small carry-on bag. "I've managed to secure an invitation to an importers conference."

She folded her arms around her middle. "How long do you intend to be gone?"

He zipped the case and placed it on a bench at the end of the footboard. "I'll return tomorrow afternoon."

"Did it occur to you to invite me along?"

He sent her a sideways glance. "You'd be bored."

"I have attended these functions with you before."

He zipped the garment bag and turned. "Yes, you have, but that was before I knew you considered me a closed-off bastard who runs at the first sign of trouble."

"You ran from me the other night. You ran after I lost the baby."

He dropped onto the edge of the mattress and forked his hands through his hair. "Perhaps you're right."

It was an admission she thought she would never hear. She sat down beside him on the bed. "I am not willing to give up on us yet, Sebastian. I would like to accompany you on this trip and we will go from there."

"Well, I've always enjoyed having a beautiful wife at my side."

That ruffled her feminine feathers. "I do not want to go as your arm ornament. I want to be there as your equal. You have never viewed me as that."

He appeared extremely confused. "Where is this coming from?"

"Well, if we want to sincerely work on our marriage, then I think it's best to be honest. Many times I have asked about the company, and you brushed me off."

"I never thought you were interested in that part of my life."

"It should be part of my life as well. After all, my father was just as immersed in the shipping world. I might not have finished my degree, but I observed all aspects of the operation. I possibly know as much about it as you do."

Now Sebastian looked skeptical. "You mean that riveting world of routes, imports and exports, and shipping containers?"

"Yes, and the importance of making connections. I am quite capable of doing that. In fact, I'll wager I will make at least two this evening if I go with you."

"I've always enjoyed a good wager. And if you succeed, I will give you whatever you desire."

"Anything?"

"Within reason."

That probably eliminated her request for a child. "And if I do not succeed?"

"I will only ask that you be patient with me. I'm not good at all this sharing-my-feelings rubbish."

An odd facet of their relationship suddenly struck

Nasira. "Do you realize that up until six months ago, we rarely ever argued?"

He seemed to mull that over for a minute. "You are absolutely right. Perhaps that is because you are perfect."

He sounded strangely sincere. "Of course that is a fallacy."

"Not to me."

"Sebastian, I know I have some habits that must drive you batty."

He rubbed his chin. "It is rather disconcerting when you rearrange my bureau drawers."

"Guilty as charged. Can you not do better than that?"

"You laugh at all my randy jokes."

"How is that an imperfection?"

"Because no one else bothers. That possibly indicates a severe lack of judgment, or perhaps bad taste."

That made her smile. "What else?"

"You bring me a drink when I'm harried after a long day."

"Again, I do not see the problem with that."

"Perhaps I prefer to fetch my own drink."

"Do you?"

He grinned. "No. The truth of the matter is, Sira, nothing you do drives me to complete distraction. Actually, that's not the truth. I'm very distracted when you walk into the room, wearing nothing but a smile, and when you wake up beside me with your hair tousled and a sleepy look on that gorgeous face. You distracted me the other night from my goal."

"Yes, I realized I ruined that goal, yet you have to

know that was not my intent. I feel horrible we did not make love."

He took her hand in his. "I meant my goal to convince you I care beyond making love to you. I want another opportunity to prove that."

"I want that as well." And she did. "And I truly want to go with you to Dallas."

"All right, as long as you understand I only have a one-bedroom suite with a king-size bed. Of course, I suppose I could see if they have another room for you."

She shook her head. "That isn't necessary."

Looking extremely pleased, he patted her thigh and stood. "The jet is waiting so you should pack. Do you have a cocktail dress for the reception?"

She came to her feet and frowned. "Do birds fly?"

He softly touched her face. "Yes, they do, and I look forward to watching you fly tonight."

But Nasira feared that by hanging on to the marriage, she might eventually fall.

Sebastian spotted her standing across the crowded room. She wore a formfitting sleeveless black silk gown with matching heels, her wrists bedecked with diamond bracelets and her sleek hair flowing down her back. Her slender hands moved gracefully as she spoke with an older gentleman who appeared completely enthralled by the conversation, and her.

Sebastian couldn't recall the last time Nasira looked so very beautiful. Correction. He could. The first night he'd seen her at an event much like the one tonight. Also on their wedding day when she had been dressed in white satin and looked like the exotic princess she was, albeit a somewhat wary princess due to their spontaneous decision to marry. Perhaps he had rescued her that day from the clutches of her father's idea of a suitable spouse, but she had saved him from a life of loneliness.

"That's one looker right there."

Sebastian turned to his right to find a portly man with thinning hair clutching a martini and staring at Nasira with lust. "That happens to be my wife."

"I know," the miscreant said. "I just spent the last thirty minutes listening to her singing your praises. By the way, I'm Milt Appleton with M.A. Imports."

Sebastian downed the rest of his scotch then eyed the man's offered hand and reluctantly shook it. "Pleasure, I'm sure." Or not.

"Anyway," Milt said. "I'm looking for a shipping company that can handle my European routes. Your girl convinced me I should consider going with you." He pulled a business card from the inside of his coat pocket. "Here's my information. Give me a shout in the next day or two."

Sebastian took the card and pocketed it. "I will be in touch soon."

Milt pointed at Nasira and narrowed his eyes. "And take care of that one. She's one in a million."

Sebastian had begun to realize the absolute accuracy of that statement. She was graceful, intelligent, resolute and reliable to a fault. She had always been there when he needed her, and he had repaid her by not being there when she had needed him. Now that he finally got it, he had to figure out what to do about it. One idea came to mind, a simple gesture that would demonstrate how much she meant to him, even if he felt he could not give her the child she still desired.

On that thought, he crossed the massive room and came to her side. "I lost track of you for a moment, darling."

She presented a smile. "I have been conversing with this lovely gentleman. Sebastian, this is Mr. Walker. Mr. Walker, my husband, Sebastian Edwards, owner and CEO of the shipping company I mentioned. Darling, Mr. Walker is quite interested in the services you have to offer."

At least this one didn't seem to be interested in the services his wife could provide. "A pleasure to meet you, Mr. Walker," he said as he stuck out his hand.

"The pleasure is all mine," the man replied. "I've given my information to your wife and we'll discuss the particulars later. Speaking of wives, I should find mine. Have a good evening, you two."

After the aged businessman hobbled away, Sebastian slid his arm around Nasira's waist. "Clearly I have lost our two-contacts wager since I was recently confronted by your first contact, the lecherous Milt."

"He's harmless," Nasira said.

"And flirtatious, I gather."

"Slightly, yet nothing I could not handle."

Sebastian glanced to his right. "Would you care to dance?"

She looked at him as if he had lost all reason. "This is not a cotillion, Sebastian. It's a cocktail party."

"I hear music coming through the speakers and I believe I spy a dance floor."

She followed his gaze toward the bar before bringing her attention back to him. "Yes, that seems to be a dance floor. With no one using it."

He clasped her hand. "Then perhaps it's time to get this dance party started." When she began to protest, he pressed her lips with a fingertip. "Let's be bold for a change. Let's show them the portrait of two people who do not give a tinker's damn what anyone thinks."

Her grin came out of hiding. "Let's."

After Sebastian guided her onto the modest wooden dance floor, Nasira walked into his arms. Yet when she noticed several people staring, she immediately went rigid.

"Relax," Sebastian whispered.

"How can I when we are making a spectacle of ourselves?"

"If anyone takes exception, it's only because they're jealous."

She reared back and leveled her gaze on him. "Jealous of two people who are clearly wacko?"

"Jealous of me for having such a remarkable wife. Jealous of you because you are the most beautiful woman in the room. In the world, in my opinion."

"If you put it that way…"

Deciding to ignore the attention, Nasira rested her cheek against Sebastian's shoulder and swayed in time to the soft sounds of a bluesy instrumental. She relished the feel of his strong arms holding her close, the aromatic scent of his cologne, his skill. She had learned that he was a great dancer the first night they had met, when he had asked her to dance at the gala, much to her father's chagrin, whose cautions had gone unheeded. When she took inventory of her life and the decision she had made, only one regret remained. A dream she might have to disregard to keep her marriage intact.

Sebastian suddenly stopped moving and only then did she realize the music had stopped, and they were now surrounded by several other couples who had taken to the floor.

Her husband presented a proud smile. "See? We have started a trend."

She laughed with pure joy. "Yes, we have."

"Shall we dance again, fair lady?"

She had something else in mind. "Actually, unless you care to stay, I would rather return to our room."

He made a show of checking his watch. "It's still early. We could have a late dinner."

Obviously he did not approve of her plan for some unknown reason. "I have had enough appetizers to last for several days."

"I have not."

"Room service is still available."

"True. I will gladly accompany you to our quarters, as long as this does not entail heavy conversation."

That would come later. Much later. "Agreed."

Reclaiming her hand, Sebastian led her through the lobby to the glass elevator that would take them to the executive floor. They entered the deserted car and took in the plethora of city lights dotting the Dallas skyline as they ascended. Unfortunately the view left Nasira breathless, and not in a welcome way.

As if he sensed her trepidation, Sebastian wrapped his arms around her from behind and held her close. "I'm right here, sweetheart."

She leaned back against him. "I know, and admittedly it is a nice panorama."

He brushed her hair aside and kissed her cheek. "At least this time you're keeping your eyes open to enjoy it."

"You take good care of me, Sebastian."

"You deserve it, Sira. You deserve everything your heart desires."

If only he could agree to give her the most important of her heart's desires. Nevertheless, she wanted to spend the evening in a lighthearted mood with no old recriminations to intrude on their time together. She also intended to bask in the glory of winning the wager about making connections at tonight's party, and if good fortune prevailed, convince him to allow her to take an active role in the business. If she could not immediately become a mother, she could certainly establish a career beyond charity work.

Those plans began to fully form as they entered the penthouse suite a few moments later. She immediately crossed the suite and walked into the bedroom with Sebastian trailing behind her. Once there, she removed her jewelry then fished through her pocket and withdrew the best part of her plan.

She turned to find her husband seated in the club chair next to the sliding glass doors leading to the veranda, his hands draped on the chair arms as if he were the king of the castle.

She approached and offered him a handful of business cards. "Here are a few more contacts."

He took the stack and looked through them before regarding her again. "You are amazing."

She smiled. "Yes. Yes I am."

He set the cards aside and returned her smile. "I'm glad you have finally come to that conclusion."

She perched on the edge of the mattress opposite him. "I am teasing. I simply struck up a few conversations and that led to mentioning the company and what we have to offer."

"We?"

She prepared to plead her case. "Yes. I assume that since I made the effort, I should be rewarded with a measure of involvement. Also, three of the contacts are women and it would only be natural that I would be the best candidate to communicate with them. Of course, I would have to be allowed access to the contracts and the shipping routes…"

He effectively cut off her thoughts when he reached over, clasped her arms, pulled her up and brought her into his lap. "You have done a superb job," he began. "And you definitely deserve to be rewarded."

She could not resist rolling her eyes. "Exactly what do you have in mind?"

He pressed a kiss on her cheek and suddenly looked very serious. "I want to give you what you want most."

She clung to hope and prepared to be disappointed.

"You know what I want most, yet you have been adamant about not giving it to me."

"I've had a change of heart."

Did she dare utter the word? No. She had learned not to assume. "Please end the suspense and say it."

"I want to give you a child."

This almost seemed too good to be true. "Are you certain?"

"Yes. As long as we adopt."

Eight

In a matter of moments, Nasira went from euphoric to disappointed. "Why is that necessary when we know we can conceive?"

"Because there are many children out there who need homes. We have that home, two in fact, and enough money to provide a solid future."

She pushed out of his lap and turned to look at him. "I truly want a baby who is a part of both of us."

Frustration clouded his expression. "You're a humanitarian, Sira. I thought the idea of giving an orphan a home would appeal to you. There are plenty in Eastern Europe."

"It does appeal to me in the future, yet I want to know how it feels to carry our child to term. As a man, perhaps you find that difficult to understand."

"I do understand, but I'm only considering your health. Why put you through the risks of another pregnancy if it's not necessary?"

She worried he would never understand. "The doctor said—"

"I know what the doctor said." Sebastian shot to his feet and began to pace. "I'm certain they said the same thing to my mother, and we know how that turned out."

Now she was completely confused. "I do not understand."

He paused to face her again. "No, you don't, because I didn't tell you the entire set of circumstances behind her death. She was pregnant because my father insisted she go against medical advice and have another child."

Shock rendered Nasira momentarily silent. "When did you learn this?"

"At the same time I learned how he was neglecting her health issues right before she died."

"More hearsay from the staff?"

He glanced away. "Yes, but I'm sure they spoke the truth."

"How can you be sure, Sebastian? You were a child yourself. Perhaps you misunderstood."

"I didn't misunderstand," he said, his tone full of anger. "I heard a reliable source say she'd had several miscarriages and each one took its toll on her. My father apparently ignored the danger and impregnated her once again. I will not put you through that."

At some point in time in the near future, Nasira vowed to find out all the details, no matter what it took. "I am not your mother, Sebastian. I have had one miscarriage and only one. I have no reason to believe I could not see the next pregnancy to term. I am willing to take that chance, and I hope you are as well."

He walked to her and clasped both her hands. "Please don't ask that of me, Sira. The thought of something happening to you is unbearable. And to know I would be responsible is inexcusable."

When she saw the vulnerability in his eyes, Nasira realized she might never break through his fear. A fear she had never witnessed in him before. She still hung on to a shred of hope that maybe with time, and more medical intervention, he would come to realize that childbirth wouldn't detrimental to her health.

She felt compelled to hold him, to tell him all would be well, yet she felt as though he had erected an invisible wall around himself. "All right. We will stray from this topic for now and attempt to enjoy the rest of our evening."

He released a rough sigh. "I'm not certain that is possible."

"It can be. Perhaps we should take a walk."

"I would prefer to stay in for the remainder of the evening."

Normally she would expect an invitation into bed. But this was not a normal situation, as evidenced by the fatigue in his tone. "If that is what you wish."

"It is."

She struggled to come up with a plan that might buoy his spirits. She returned to their mutual past and better days for inspiration. "I have a proposition."

His smile arrived slowly. "I've always enjoyed a good proposition."

The bad boy billionaire had come back to life. "This involves dessert."

"Interesting you should use that term."

The real Sebastian had arrived, and she felt a modicum of relief. "I meant dessert as in cake, on the veranda. We have not done that in a very long time."

He turned her hands over and kissed both her wrists. "Perhaps it's time we begin to recapture what we've lost."

Nasira chose to interpret Sebastian's statement as reclaiming the routines that had once given them pleasure, aside from lovemaking. She gently wrested her hands away and walked into the living area to retrieve the menu.

While she flipped through the selections, Sebastian came up behind her and peered over her shoulder. "The raspberry truffle cheesecake looks good," he said. "Shall I order that for us?"

She closed the menu, laid it aside on the desk and then turned, which placed her in extremely close proximity to him. So close she could barely catch her breath. "Actually, I would prefer to order for myself."

"My apologies. I've already forgotten one important lesson—let Sira make her own culinary decisions."

In light of the sexy gleam in his eye, she would forgive him this slight slipup. "Apology accepted. And I would like the sampler that includes several choices."

He frowned. "Are you certain you can handle that much food?"

"I can because I am suddenly starving."

Oddly, her appetite had increased over the past two days. In fact, the last time she had been this hungry...

That was not possible, not after only one time. Not so soon. She was being silly. Optimism over resolving their issues was simply driving her cravings. That had to be the case.

Seated at the small table on the hotel's veranda, Sebastian watched his wife eat with total abandon and couldn't quite believe his eyes. "In all our years together, I have never seen you entirely clean your plate."

Nasira dabbed at her mouth with the napkin and set it aside. "It was very tasty."

"Apparently. Should I order you more?"

That earned him a frown. "I could not eat another bite. I believe the country air is making me very hungry."

"Sira, we're in the city."

"True." She shifted in the chair and studied the horizon. "I had no idea Dallas would be so metropolitan."

"Did you believe you'd find people riding around the city streets on horseback?"

"Of course not. However, I did see a horse-drawn carriage downstairs."

"Perhaps we should make use of one."

She brought her attention back to him. "It is rather late."

"Not too late to enjoy the sights."

"I thought you wanted to stay in."

Sebastian was so restless, he wasn't certain what

he wanted, except to be close to his wife. "It will be a nice diversion," he said as he pushed back from the table and stood.

"All right." Nasira came to her feet and pointed at him. "No funny business."

Damn. "I only wish to have the honor of your company." And that was a colossal lie, though he vowed to respect her wishes.

By the time they reached the hotel lobby and walked out the revolving doors, the sidewalks weren't as crowded as Sebastian had expected. Fortunately he spotted a carriage stopped near the curb only a few meters away. He approached the gentleman dressed in Western garb positioned in the driver's seat. "Good evening, sir. Are you currently for hire?"

The man stared down at him. "Actually, I was just about to head to the house."

Sebastian withdrew his wallet and offered the man two hundred-dollar bills. "Will this make it worth your while?"

The driver eyed the money for a moment. "My wife's got dinner waiting."

He pulled out another hundred. "Now you can buy your wife dinner."

"I s'pose I could take you a few blocks."

Greedy scoundrel. "I would think that amount would buy us a few kilometers."

Nasira elbowed him in the side. "*Darling*, the poor man wants to go home to his wife."

Her compassion had him looking like a pitiless cad.

"Of course. My apologies. I only want to show my brand-new bride a memorable evening."

The driver grabbed the reins and sneered. "Then let's get this show on the road so you can get on with the honeymoon. Just don't get it on in my carriage."

"For three hundred dollars, I should be allowed to prance naked in a parade," Sebastian muttered as he helped Nasira up into the seat.

After they settled in, he draped an arm around her shoulder. "Was that jab to my ribs necessary?"

"Were your derisive comments necessary?"

"The reprobate seemed determined to stiff me."

"He clearly holds his wife above work. And what compelled you to claim we've recently married?"

His faults had been laid bare. "Well, in a way I feel as if we are newlyweds. We've discovered quite a bit about each other over the past few weeks."

She mulled that over for a moment. "It is odd to think that two people who have spent so many years together would still have the capacity to learn more about each other."

He had told her things he had never uttered to another soul. Details he had planned to take to his grave. Yet he did feel less burdened knowing she now understood why he did not want her risking carrying his child after her previous miscarriage. "Let's promise that we'll continue this unusual pattern in the upcoming weeks."

She laid her head on his shoulder. "A stellar plan."

As they rode through the streets of Dallas, serenaded by the clip-clop of horse hooves, Sebastian tugged Nasira closer to him. Without a blanket to conceal them, she was not in danger of any funny business, as she had so aptly put it. That did little to quash his desire for her. That did not stop him from rubbing her shoulder with one hand and tracing slow circles on her thigh. She responded by making small sounds that served to heighten his need for her, and drove him to kiss her thoroughly. And she kissed him back with enough passion to make him want to say to hell with propriety, pull her panties down and take right there in front of the entire town...

The sound of applause forced them apart. There was a crowd gathered at the corner where they had stopped for a traffic light. Sebastian did what any good Brit would do—stood, executed a bow and gave them a royal wave.

When he settled back in the seat, Nasira began to laugh and he followed suit. Once they recovered, he leaned and nuzzled her neck. "You smell like lavender. Is it a new perfume?"

"You gave it to me for my birthday."

Unfortunately that purchase had been made three months ago by Stella when he had forgotten. "Ah yes. Now I remember."

She swatted his arm. "You do not, but you are forgiven."

"For everything?"

"For now."

He refused to ruin the mood by asking her to elaborate. Instead, he decided to put all his cards on the table at the risk of rejection. "Would you mind if I take you back to the room and ravish you?"

"Not in the least."

That had been much too easy, in his opinion. "Really?"

"Yes."

"Should I perhaps define ravish?"

"I assume you mean you wish to remove my clothes, take me to bed and have your wicked way with me."

"Precisely."

"My answer is still yes."

Shifting against the building pressure in his groin, Sebastian tapped the driver on the shoulder to garner his attention. "Kind sir, please return us to the hotel as quickly as possible and you will earn a sizeable tip."

The man glanced over his shoulder. "We've barely been three blocks."

Sebastian had no desire to argue the point. "Unless you want your bloody carriage serving as a boudoir, you will do as I say."

The jerk had the gall to grin. "You got it."

Sebastian settled back against the seat and smiled. "Let the faux honeymoon commence."

Nasira worried they might not make it past the elevator before clothes began to come off. Her resolute husband somehow maintained enough control to refrain from disrobing until they reached the suite. On the way to the bedroom, they began shedding attire and shoes and by the time they fell back on the mattress, they were entirely naked and completely entangled.

Sebastian suddenly stilled and rose up. "I want to slow this down. I want this to last and if we keep going, it will be over in a matter of minutes."

She pushed a wayward lock of hair from his forehead. "You will receive no objections from me."

He rolled her onto her side so that she was facing the glass doors and moved against her back.

"Do you recall our first night?" he asked as he ran his palm over the curve of her hip.

"How could I forget? I was so very nervous, and you were so gentle."

"You were also a virgin, something you didn't tell me until right before that pivotal moment."

"I wanted to seem worldly. I did not want you to know I was so inexperienced."

"You also didn't want me to know you'd never had an orgasm. You told me the morning after. I've always been curious why you had never pleasured yourself."

"That would have been considered forbidden."

"And have you experimented since we've been married?"

"Never."

"Not even over the past few months?"

She sensed his sudden bout of guilt. "No. I only wanted you."

He slid his hand to the inside of her thigh. "And I made you wait for months."

"Having you touch me was worth the wait."

As they lay there in silence, Sebastian plying her with gentle strokes, the lights of the city illuminated the darkened room, making the atmosphere seem highly sensual and romantic. Nasira closed her eyes, taking in the ambience and willing the climax to remain at bay. Yet her efforts proved futile, and she again gave in to nature's course and her husband's skill as she experienced blessed relief.

So deep was the blissful aftermath that Nasira wasn't aware Sebastian had left her until she heard the sound of him tearing a condom wrapper, a reminder that he still was not willing to conceive a child. She shifted to her back and wrenched the negative thoughts from her mind. And when he returned, she welcomed him into her arms and her body. Feeling the play of his muscles beneath her palms, she held on tightly as he moved inside her, deeper and deeper, faster and faster. She listened to the sound of his ragged breaths and knew the exact moment when his own orgasm took over. Then he whispered her name.

After a time, he rolled to his back and took her with him, their bodies fitting together like a perfect human puzzle. During the next span of silence, she expected to hear his steady breathing, indicating he had fallen asleep. Instead, he played with her hair and showered her face with gentle kisses.

She was beginning to give in to the lull of sleep herself when he sighed and rested his lips against her ear. "I love you, Sira."

Never in her wildest dreams had she ever believed she would hear those words, though she had secretly hoped that someday she would. Even now she believed she might be dreaming. She said the only thing she could manage to say. The words she had kept harbored in her heart for fear that if she voiced them, she would be lost to this enigmatic man forever.

"I love you, too."

While Sebastian continued to hold her close, Nasira felt as if all her wishes had come true. All but one. Yet now that she knew her husband truly loved her, would she be foolish to believe she might be granted the child she had always wanted? Perhaps that would be too much to ask, yet as she recalled both Violet's and Fiona's claim that Royal, Texas, was a place bestowed with magic, she desperately wanted to believe she could have some magic of her own.

Time had passed quickly since their return to the Shakirs' ranch. Sebastian and Nasira had shared three wonderful and blissful weeks full of meaningful conversation and memorable moments. She had never felt so cherished, or so loved, by her husband.

Sebastian had showered her with small gifts, had made love to her often and had barely tended to business. Following Violet and Rafe's wedding in two days, she planned to return to London with her husband and continue their marriage with an eye toward a bright future, even though he had given her no indication he wanted to work on having a baby. Yet she believed that with a bit more gentle persuasion, he would eventually come around, and hopefully she was not giving way to false optimism. If not, she would have to decide if she would be willing to adopt and give up the dream of feeling her own child growing inside her.

After finishing her morning tea in the kitchen, Nasira took the cup to the sink, and immediately felt two strong arms encircling her from behind. "How dare you leave me alone in bed?" Sebastian asked in a teasing tone.

She turned and kissed his unshaven chin. "If you recall, I am meeting Violet for breakfast."

He slid his hand beneath her blue tailored blouse and cupped her breast through her lace bra. "Do you need a ride?"

"I thought I would drive myself."

He rimmed the shell of her ear with his tongue. "That wasn't the ride I had in mind."

Of course not. "I do not want to keep Violet waiting. She is anxious enough with all the wedding chaos."

Sebastian slid his hands over Nasira's hips and pressed against her. "What time do you expect to return?"

She saw afternoon delight in her near future. "I assume in few hours. We have to go over the final details and that could take some time."

He scowled. "The blasted wedding is spoiling my fun."

She patted his pajama-covered bottom and stepped aside. "You have had more than your share of fun of late."

He leaned back against the counter, bringing his bare torso into full view and sparking Nasira's imagination. "If I can interest you in more fun, let me know. In the meantime, while you ladies are discussing catering and flowers, I shall be making a few calls to prospective American clients."

Before she forgot her duties and caved in to her own cravings, Nasira grabbed her bag from the counter and kissed her husband squarely on the mouth. "I should be back before lunch. Be naked and waiting in the bed."

He grinned and winked. "If you give me advance warning, I'll be waiting naked in the foyer. Or if you allow me to drive you, we could have a quick roll in the car."

"Definitely a cad," she said as she headed to the entry, plagued with visions of Sebastian taking her down on the plush rug or in the sedan. Or both.

Nasira fished the keys from the pocket of her dress and slid into the driver's seat, thankful Sebastian had encouraged her to learn to drive on the correct side of the road for when they returned for visits. She liked the thought of coming back to Texas to see her brother's baby and perhaps by then she would be carrying one of her own. Or perhaps it was much too soon to hope for that blessing.

Setting those nagging concerns aside, she navigated the country road with relative ease and arrived at the Royal Diner to find Violet's new Jaguar—a wedding gift from Rafe—parked in the lot near the street. Nasira selected the empty space beside the sedan, turned off the ignition and regarded her watch. The fact she was fifteen minutes late flew in the face of her usual punctual self.

After she entered the restaurant, Nasira caught sight of Violet and Mac's assistant, Andrea Beaumont, seated at a small table in the corner. She strode across the room at a fast clip, until a bout of dizziness caused her to slow her pace. Clearly she was in need of sustenance, yet the scents emanating from the kitchen served to make her a bit queasy.

"I am so sorry for my tardiness," she said as she settled into the chair across from Violet and set her purse at her feet. "I awoke a bit later than planned."

"I hope you had a good reason," Violet said with a teasing smile.

"I do too," Andrea chimed in. "Did your handsome husband detain you?"

Nasira felt heat rise to her face. "Actually no, but that is only because I climbed out of bed before he roused."

"In that case, you should have hung around a little longer," Violet said. "I take it you and Sebastian are mending fences and maybe making a baby in the process?"

If only the last part were true. "We are making very good progress. Now what have I missed in regard to the wedding plans?"

Violet studied the notepad before her. "Actually, I'm fairly sure everything is in place. The menu has been finalized and the flowers have arrived from Hawaii. The cake is going to be gorgeous and the tent should be set up by two. Andrea arranged for a quartet to play during the ceremony and she's confirmed Rafe and Mac's tuxedos are ready to go."

"Now we only have to make sure the groom arrives on time," Andrea added.

With the arrangements already taken care of, Nasira wondered why she had been invited to the lunch today. "What can I do?" she asked.

Violet grinned. "Make sure the groom arrives on time."

Nasira returned her smile. "I can certainly do that, although I believe my brother will be there early, anxiously waiting to claim his bride. What time would you like us to arrive?"

"I'll be getting dressed at the house around noon," Violet said. "I could definitely use your help zipping my dress, if I can get it zipped."

Andrea laid a hand on Violet's arm. "Stop it. You're barely showing."

Violet patted her slightly distended belly. "My baby bump is much bigger, and I'm sure the breakfast I'm planning to eat isn't going to help." She slid a menu in front of Nasira. "I highly recommend the buttermilk pancakes with a side of bacon."

Nasira's stomach lurched at the thought. "I believe I will have toast and tea."

Andrea pushed away from the table and stood. "You girls enjoy your meal. Unfortunately Mac has a full schedule today so I'm going to have to settle for coffee and a granola bar I have stashed in my desk."

Violet frowned. "Tell my brother to stop being such a slave driver."

Andrea released a cynical laugh. "That would be like telling a cowboy to give up his spurs," she said as she headed out.

As soon as Andrea left, Violet shook her head and sighed. "I'll be so glad when those two finally admit they want a relationship beyond business. Mac is so stubborn he can't see the forest for the trees. I really want to shake some sense into him."

"Most men are stubborn," Nasira said. "My husband included."

"But he's coming around, right?" Violet asked.

"Yes, he is." Nasira wanted to delve into more detail but decided not to burden her brother's bride with her problems. "How have you been feeling with all the wedding stress?"

Violet took a sip of water and leaned back in the chair. "Better than I expected. The morning, noon and night sickness has subsided for the most part. I could still fall asleep on my feet at times, which I've learned is typical."

Nasira recalled the fatigue, along with the overwhelming sadness after her loss. "It is normal."

"I'm so sorry for being insensitive, Nasira," Violet said, her tone laced with sympathy. "I know how difficult it's been since your miscarriage."

"It's all right, Violet. Enough time has passed where I no longer fall apart around pregnant women."

"Are you sure?"

"I am sure. I would never want you to feel you have to be guarded around me when it comes to your pregnancy. In fact, I am thrilled to have a new niece or nephew. And I would enjoy living vicariously through you until I have my own child. After all, you can give me advice when that happens." *If* that happened.

"I'm personally looking forward to the next phase," Violet continued. "I have a friend who claims she couldn't get enough sex, and I know that will thrill

Rafe. Of course, the best part about being pregnant is…" She leaned forward and whispered, "No period."

No period…

The comment prompted Nasira to grab her cell phone from her bag and retrieve the calendar app. After she scanned the dates and did a mental countdown, she was overcome with panic when she should have been overcome with joy.

"Are you all right, Nasira?"

She raised her gaze to Violet. "I… I think…"

"You think what?"

"I might be pregnant."

And if that were true, she could only imagine what that possibility would entail. Perhaps stress had been the cause of her missing her period. Perhaps it would be best to wait a bit longer to find out the truth.

Nine

"You're definitely pregnant, Nasira."

A short while later, Nasira found herself at Rafe and Violet's home, holding the second of two positive pregnancy tests in one hand, steeped in shock. "I cannot believe this."

Violet wrested the plastic stick from her grip and set it on the vanity. "Believe it. I think taking a third is a bit of overkill."

Nasira pinched the bridge of her nose and closed her eyes. "How am I to tell Sebastian?"

"Easy. 'Sebastian, you're going to be a daddy.'"

If only it were that simple. If only he would embrace fatherhood. If only... "He will not be happy about this."

"What makes you believe that?"

Nasira opened her eyes to Violet's concerned expression. "It is very complicated. My husband is complicated."

"I can do complicated, Nasira. Now let's go into the living room and you can explain."

Nasira aimlessly followed her future sister-in-law into the parlor and settled in beside her on the sofa. After taking a cleansing breath, she began the arduous explanation by recounting Sebastian's concerns for her safety, his bittersweet memories of his mother, his reluctance to be like his father. She ended her explanation in a haze of tears, saying, "I am worried he will never accept the news at this point."

"He has no choice," Violet said with certainty. "It might take some time, but after he sees you're totally healthy and happy, he'll get used to the idea. And as soon as he holds your baby the first time, he'll wonder why he wasted so much energy worrying over nothing."

Nasira wished she could be so confident. "I hope you are right, Violet."

"And on the off chance I'm not, what are you going to do?"

Nasira had yet to make any solid decisions in that regard. "I suppose I will wait and see how Sebastian reacts when I deliver the news."

Violet took her hand. "I know it's tempting to put it off as long as possible, but the sooner you tell him, the sooner you'll know how to prepare for the future."

"I would rather hop a plane to Bermuda and bask on the beach."

"And I wish I could wear normal jeans again."

They exchanged a smile and a quick embrace before

Nasira came to her feet. "I so very much appreciate your counsel. Please wish me luck."

"Good luck." Violet stood and drew her into another embrace. "That's what family is for. And if your husband acts like a jerk, you know you always have a place here with us."

"I would never want to impose."

"You wouldn't be imposing. I'm sure Rafe would be thrilled to have his pregnant little sister and wife hanging around, driving him insane with sporadic hormonal outbursts."

Nasira tried to laugh yet it sounded hollow. "That would be the last thing my brother would want, having his younger sibling residing under the same roof while he is in the honeymoon phase with his new bride."

Violet's expression went suddenly serious. "He's very protective of you, Nasira. I'd hate to think what he might do if he knew about Sebastian's attitude toward fatherhood."

The thought made Nasira even more anxious. "Promise me you will not tell him."

"I promise," Violet said. "And you promise me you'll call as soon as Sebastian knows. If he throws a fit, get in the car and come here so he can cool down."

Nasira sincerely wanted to believe that would not be necessary, yet she found comfort in the offer. At least she would not be alone should Sebastian decide to walk out on their marriage. "I will, and thank you for being such a grand friend. I suppose I should go now and face the music."

"Nasira, in my heart of hearts," Violet began, "I believe everything will work out well. Sebastian might be snake-bit in the baby department, but it's obvious he loves you very much."

Nasira wanted to have faith in that as well, but her concerns only increased as they walked out the door into the warm May night.

"One more thing, Nasira," Violet said when they reached the sedan. "Every child is a gift and if Sebastian can't see that, then he's a fool. Don't let him allow you to think this is all your fault."

Nasira touched the place that housed her unborn child. "You are right. This baby is all I have ever wanted." And could be all she would have if her love for Sebastian, and his love for her, proved not to be enough to overcome their differences.

As she drove toward the ranch, Nasira recognized she would need a good dose of courage, and perhaps ammunition, for the upcoming debate she would surely have with her husband. On that thought, she pulled the sedan to the side of the road to make a call that could provide her with the information she needed. A fact-finding mission that could possibly hold the key to the past, and perhaps the fate of her future.

She withdrew the cell to input the number and waited. When she heard the familiar voice, she drew in a deep breath and exhaled slowly. "Stella, this is Nasira. I am in dire need of your help."

"What ever is wrong, dear?"

Everything. "Nothing really. I simply need to know all the details of Sebastian's mother's death."

She was met with momentary silence before Stella spoke again. "I am not at liberty—"

"Please, Stella. This is of the utmost importance. I need to know. Sebastian needs to know."

"Then you will need to speak to James about it."

That posed a grave dilemma. "Do you believe he's able to tell me?"

"Oh yes. He often leaves the present, yet he is very much suspended in the past."

"I do not want this to upset him."

"I assure you, it will. It does every time he goes back to that time, and he does so often."

"I would never want to cause James any distress, but this is very important." Even though going behind Sebastian's back could incur his wrath, and only make matters worse. Still, she had to take that chance in light of learning she was pregnant.

A span of silence passed before Stella spoke again. "All right, but be quick about it, and if he becomes too upset, I implore you to end the conversation."

"I promise I will."

"Then wait a moment and I will bring the phone to him."

Nasira heard indistinguishable sounds then James's careworn voice saying, "Hello, Nasira. Stella tells me you want to talk about my Martha. She was a jewel of a woman…."

She listened patiently as her father-in-law extolled the virtues of his late wife, and with great interest when he finally arrived at the fateful day in question. The information was both stunning and troubling. By the time the conversation ended, Nasira was no less clear on what she should tell Sebastian. The truth could truly set him free, or sever their marriage once and for all.

She had no choice but to reveal everything, every last dreadful detail, and prepare for the predictable fallout after she confessed to him she was pregnant.

Sebastian was beside himself. Nasira hadn't called to say why she had been detained, and her phone was going directly to voice mail. That caused him great concern. He should have given her a ride to the diner. He should have rented a second car. What if she had been in an accident, or at the very least, found herself lost on some dilapidated Texas back road? If she didn't arrive soon, he would contact the law and organize a search party.

After he heard the front door open a few minutes later, though, he finally relaxed…until he noticed the distressed look on Nasira's face when she entered the great room. He shot off the sofa, his nerves on edge. "What happened to you?"

She tossed her bag on the coffee table and collapsed in the club chair across from him. "The meeting with Violet went longer than planned."

It was so unlike his wife to blatantly lie, but she had. "I called Violet. She said you left the diner an hour ago."

Nasira averted her gaze. "I suppose I did at that. I was on the phone and lost track of time."

He was plagued by an immediate surge of jealousy. "Were you talking to that McCallum fellow?"

She nailed him with a glare. "Do not be absurd, Sebastian. I haven't spoken with Mac since the night you arrived."

Only minimally relieved, Sebastian lowered onto the sofa and leaned forward to look for any sign of deception in her eyes. "Who else in town would you be talking to if not him?"

She kicked off her sandals and curled her legs beneath her. "I never said I spoke to anyone from Royal. For your information, I was in touch with London."

He couldn't seem to contain his sarcasm. "It's no wonder the call took so long if you talked to the entire city. Could you possibly be more specific?"

"If you must know, I spoke with Stella."

He worried the news might involve his father, and it might not be good. "What did she want?"

"Actually, I called her."

"To check in on our status?"

"To gather the details of your mother's death, which I did."

He waffled between resentment over the intrusion to borderline anger. "Forgive me if I'm feeling somewhat betrayed. The least you could have done was tell me your plans to contact her."

"I understand, but I felt it was of the utmost importance you know the whole truth."

"I don't see why any of it should matter now."

"It does, Sebastian, and you'll realize why as soon as I tell you what I've learned with your stepmother's assistance."

For some reason, he experienced trepidation over the possible contents of the conversation. "I'm quite surprised Stella would tell you what she knows, if she really knows anything pertinent beyond what I've heard."

"I learned the facts from your father, not Stella."

The revelation took Sebastian aback. "My father doesn't remember what he had for dinner."

"He does still remember the past, and quite well."

Sebastian couldn't argue with that observation. "I'm not certain I care to hear his version of the truth."

"You are going to hear it," she said almost forcefully. "And I believe you will be glad you did."

He believed she would be sorely disappointed. "I'll be the judge of that, but please, continue. I enjoy a good fairy tale now and then."

She shifted her weight slightly, a certain sign of her uneasiness. "First of all, your mother was not pregnant at the time of her death."

"Of course he would say that—"

"She *was* pregnant not long before her death," Nasira proclaimed before he could finish his sentence, then added, "A fact unbeknownst to everyone, including your father."

Sebastian allowed the astonishment to subside and logic to come into the picture. "I have a difficult time believing a straightforward woman like my mother would conceal a pregnancy from anyone, let alone her husband."

A strange look passed over Nasira's face. "She had her reasons, Sebastian. Some might say good reasons under the circumstances."

He saw no excuse for blatant dishonesty, and he had a difficult time believing his own mother—the one he remembered—would engage in serious subterfuge. "And what would those reasons be?"

"She kept the pregnancy hidden because your father was adamant she not have another child due to her multiple miscarriages. He sided with the physicians, not your mother, although he claimed that was agony. He loved her so much he hated not giving her a baby."

He had never known his father to agonize over anything other than the state of the global economy. "Clearly James was not without fault in the matter since I assume he was present when she conceived."

"Yes, but she lied about using birth control because she wanted another baby that badly."

Exactly what Nasira had initially done to him, as if history were bent on repeating itself. "Did the pregnancy directly cause her demise?"

"Indirectly. She apparently had another miscarriage and chose not to tell anyone, including her physician. That led to a lethal infection and subsequently, her untimely death."

He took a few moments to digest the information, then summarily rejected it. "It would be just like my father to twist the truth to relieve himself of all culpability."

"He has no reason to lie, Sebastian. Stella told me he has lived with horrible guilt since the day your mother passed away. He blames himself for her decision to keep quiet about the baby. He believes if he had not been so set against her conceiving, she would have told him about the pregnancy and he could have prevented her death."

He acknowledged the scenario made sense, yet he had trouble trusting the source. "I'm still having a great deal of difficulty believing my father remained totally in the dark."

"Stella suspected you would, so she offered to give you the official certification."

"That only confirms the cause of death, not my father's claims."

Nasira impaled him with a glare the likes of which he'd never witnessed. "If you will stop being such a buffoon and search your soul, you might finally realize that your mother was not a saint, and your father is not Satan."

He suddenly felt extremely drained. "I'll attempt to come to terms with the information, but I cannot promise I will feel any differently."

He could tell by the lift of her chin and the defiance in her eyes she wasn't quite finished with the lecture. "It is high time you call an end to your suspicions and resentment. If you don't, you will possibly regret the decision after it is too late to make amends with James. Believe me, that is a burden you will not want to bear."

Sebastian wanted to debate the pros and cons of forgiveness, but his emotions were too tangled in turmoil. He rested against the sofa and feigned a calm demeanor. "Did you enjoy your time with Violet?"

Nasira's dark eyes widened with disbelief. "You wish to know about my day after what I revealed?"

"I see no point in dwelling on the past."

"I do if it relates to our future, and our present situation."

"This information has no bearing on us, Sira, aside from the fact it does reinforce why it's not wise for you to become pregnant again."

"As I have said before, I am not your mother. I am healthy and able to bear more children. Women have babies every day without incident. Life holds no guarantees and comes with a certain amount of—"

"Risk," he finished for her. "I understand that, but it's a risk I don't care to take with your well-being. And if you don't mind, I would like to move off this subject for now."

She lowered her eyes and clasped her hands tightly in her lap. "I cannot discard my worries, Sebastian. Not after what I discovered today."

Concern came crashing down on him as he braced for confirmation of what he suspected she was about to say. "Please tell me you're not pregnant."

She centered her gaze on his. "I am pregnant, and I am thrilled. I hope you will put aside your fears and celebrate the news."

Celebrate? He came off the couch, laced his hands behind his neck and began to pace like a caged cougar. "How can you expect me to be happy after what you've told me about my mother?"

"I knew I was taking a chance by unveiling the truth, yet I had to be forthright."

He spun around to confront her. "That truth only cements my apprehension."

"Your mother chose to become pregnant against medical advice and your father's protests. She also chose not to seek appropriate treatment after she lost the baby, and in turn inadvertently caused her own death due to her deception. In a way I understand—"

"Of course you would," he said, noticeable anger in his tone. "I imagine you would do the same."

Fury turned her features to stone. "I would not do the same, and I cannot fathom why you would believe I would risk my life to have a baby if I had been told the cost would be so high. But I have not been told that, Sebastian. On the contrary, the doctor said I have every reason to believe this time will be different."

"And what if it's not? What if you lose another child? Worse still, what if you lose your life?"

She finally rose from the sofa. "I refuse to buy into your pessimism and fears. I choose to be optimistic and hopeful. If you cannot join me in that optimism, then there is no hope for us at all."

He experienced a different fear. "What are you saying?"

"I am saying go back to London, Sebastian. If you do not want this child, and clearly you do not, then I cannot be with a man who will not support me during my pregnancy. I would prefer to be surrounded by people who will be happy to provide that support. I have that here with Rafe and Violet."

"I need time to think." Time to assess the possibilities.

She picked up her purse, withdrew the bracelet with the rattle charm he had given her all those months ago and laid it on the table before him, as if she was bent on wounding him further. "Then think, but I warn you not to take too long. In the meantime, I am going to stay with Rafe until you decide what you want. I respectfully request you not attempt to contact me until you've made up your mind. I will have someone return the car later this evening."

As he watched his wife walk away, Sebastian experienced a strong sense of déjà vu. Her departure from London a brief month ago had come with the same demand not to contact her. Then, too, he had suffered an emotional pain that stole his breath and his resolve. With his overriding fear of losing Nasira, he had definitely cemented that self-fulfilling prophecy he'd been so concerned about.

He wasn't the kind of man who would abandon his child, provided that child came to be, yet he worried his wife had already abandoned any expectations of salvaging their marriage.

If he did not come to terms with impending fatherhood, and learn to embrace it, he risked saying goodbye to his beautiful Nasira for good.

He had too much to consider, and too little time.

"Have you heard from your worthless husband?"

Seated in the chair next to the window, Nasira glanced up from the book she was pretending to read, steeling herself against her brother's consternation. "Have I?"

He moved from the doorway and perched on the bench at the end of the bed. "If I knew, I would not have asked."

"If my memory serves me correctly, you failed to tell me Sebastian called when I arrived here. How can

I trust that you have not thwarted his attempts to contact me this time?"

"I assure you he has not called and if he had, I would have informed you immediately. I have learned my lesson in that regard."

She highly doubted that. "I truly do not want you to worry about my situation during what should be a joyous time for you and Violet. Are you looking forward to the wedding tomorrow?"

"I am looking forward to having Violet back in my bed. I do not understand the tradition involving withholding the bride from the groom before the wedding."

"It is believed that sleeping with the bride the night before the wedding will invite bad luck."

"It only invites sexual frustration."

Spoken like a man. "Has she left yet?"

"No. She is still packing her suitcases while Mac remains downstairs, growing increasingly impatient. What will you do if Sebastian returns to London without contacting you?"

Nasira refused to give up on him yet. "I am trying not to entertain that possibility."

"Regardless, I will contact Nolan Dane after Violet and I return from our honeymoon. He's a lawyer here in Royal who used to work for me."

"I do not need a barrister." At least not presently.

"You might in the future. He will provide a reference for a family law attorney should you decide to pursue a divorce. Preferably a high-profile attorney to ensure you will receive an equitable share of your husband's assets. One who has experience dealing with international divorce."

She tossed her book onto the side table and sighed. "I do not need Sebastian's money, Rafe. I have more than enough left of my inheritance."

"That is your decision."

"Yes, it is."

"At the very least he should be required to support the child."

She should not be surprised that Violet had told Rafe about the baby. Somewhat disappointed, yes, but not at all shocked. "I see you have been talking to your fiancée."

"Do not blame Violet, Nasira. I pressed her for information when you arrived on our doorstep, looking as though you had lost your dearest friend. She had no choice but to reveal the details to put my mind at ease, although she did not accomplish that goal."

"You need not worry, brother," Nasira said. "I will manage on my own if necessary."

Rafe took on an angry guise. "I would like to seek out Sebastian and tell him—"

"You will not say a word, Rafiq. This is not your concern."

"You have always been my concern, my petite pearl."

She smiled at the brotherly term of endearment. "I am no longer your life, Rafe. Violet is. Your unborn child is."

He rose from the bench, crossed the space between them and pressed a kiss to her forehead. "You will al-

ways be a part of my life. I will always be there to protect you if your husband refuses to do so."

She had to learn to accept that Sebastian could be
absent from her world forever. That she might never
converse with him again. Hold him again. Make love
with him again…

The shrill of the doorbell thrust her thoughts back to
the present. The sound of the deep, endearing voice de-
manding he see her sent her shattered heart on a sprint.

Had he come to tell her he intended to stay, or to say
farewell for all eternity?

Ten

As his brother-in-law descended the staircase, stood in the opening to the parlor Sebastian prepared to be thrown out on his arse. Yet when Nasira followed not far behind, sporting a plain cotton blouse, light blue slacks and a champion scowl, he sensed she would prefer to do the honors herself. He would accept that fate. He deserved it.

He glanced to his right to see Violet and her brother, Mac, Sebastian's former nemesis, seated on the sofa as if they planned to preside over a kangaroo court with him playing the defendant. Rafe brushed past him and claimed the overstuffed chair adjacent to the settee, not bothering to hide his disdain for his sister's spouse.

Nasira remained in the foyer, her arms folded beneath her breasts, looking every bit the hanging judge. "Well?"

"May I speak with you in private, Sira?" he asked with forced civility. "It's extremely important."

She regarded the curious onlookers before bringing her attention back to him. "Whatever you need to say, you may say it in front of my family and friends."

She had turned his privacy plan on its proverbial ear, and he would have to accept it, even if it meant an unwelcome audience. "You're absolutely right. Your friends and family are most welcome to witness what I have to say. I only hope they support my decision."

Her shoulders immediately tensed. "I assume that decision involves your return to London."

Wrong. He took both her hands in his. "I'm not going anywhere without you. I'm here to humbly ask you to forgive all my faults."

"Such as?"

He'd compiled a laundry list that was too long to recite now, so he would concentrate on those which would matter most to her. "Forgive me for periodically leaving my towel on the floor after I shower. Forgive me for leading you to believe that I think you're not capable of being involved in the business, because you are, and I welcome your input. Above all, I beg you to forgive me for being such a bloody, controlling coward."

"I have never said you are a coward."

A point in his favor. "Perhaps not, but I wouldn't blame you if you thought it." He paused to draw a breath. "The truth of the matter is, I have fought with men twice my size—"

"Seriously?" Violet interjected.

"I'd believe it," Mac added.

Rafe cleared his throat. "Let the man continue. Violet needs her rest and at this rate, we will be here until midnight."

Violet leaned over and patted her husband's cheek. "Thank you, honey."

"As I was saying," Sebastian continued, "I've been in several situations that required bravery, but the thought of being responsible for a tiny, helpless creature frankly scares the hell out of me."

He studied Nasira's eyes and saw a glimpse of understanding, or so he assumed. "Sebastian, you are in charge of a major corporation. I am confident you can handle fatherhood with the same aplomb."

"Except for the dirty diapers maybe," Mac said, earning him a look from Rafe.

"I can only promise I will try," Sebastian said sincerely. "But what I lack in skill, I will make up in the willingness to learn."

Instead of falling into his arms, she frowned. "Why the sudden turnaround, Sebastian?"

He should have realized she wouldn't make this easy on him. "I spent hours thinking about what you said. Life isn't without risk, but I'm willing to take that risk with you in light of the reward. I've also spoken with Stella and my father. I've come to the conclusion that I've wasted many years resenting a man without just cause, and I will never know true peace unless I learn to forgive his faults. And I hope you forgive mine. In reality, I'm very much like him, and only part of that is learned behavior. The other part is genetic."

He couldn't seem to even coax a slight smile from her. "Will you be able to love our baby?"

More than she would know. More than he could express. "I vow to love our child as much as I love our child's mother."

When he pulled the bracelet from his pocket in an effort to confirm his commitment, and placed it on Nasira's wrist, his wife finally smiled. "That is all I needed to know. And I love you, too. I forgive you all your faults, if you will forgive mine as well."

His spirits soared like a hawk. "You're perfect, Sira. But I need to warn you, you'll have to be patient with me. I'm going to worry about you every moment of every day during your pregnancy. I'm definitely going to be ridiculously overprotective and I'll be gauging your every move—"

"Shut up and kiss me, Sebastian."

She would get no argument from him. As he took her in his arms and kissed her soundly, for the first time in many years, he felt entirely at peace. Once they parted, he realized the room had cleared out as though he was a randy rock star giving a bad performance. "Would you care to accompany me back to our rented ranch?"

She hid a yawn behind her hand. "Gladly. I am so exhausted. I could not sleep without you by my side."

Neither could he. "Rest assured I will respect your need for sleep. You will have to get more of it to remain healthy."

She slid her arms around his waist and sent him a sly grin. "Actually, I am not that tired, nor am I fragile."

No, she was not, and he realized he had known that all along. "Well then, Mrs. Edwards, let us away to our borrowed bed."

"That sounds like a very good plan, Mr. Edwards."

They made love once during the night, and again in the morning. As the first light of dawn streamed through the slightly parted curtains, Nasira rested her cheek on Sebastian's chest and listened to the strong beat of his heart as she basked in the afterglow of remarkable lovemaking...and much-needed hope for their future together.

Sebastian's steady strokes on her back threatened to lull her to sleep, but she awoke completely when he shifted slightly. "You know what I like best about your pregnancy?" he asked.

"I know what I like best," she murmured. "I can avoid tight clothing for nine months."

"You would look good in a gunny sack, Nasira. I personally enjoy not having to wear another bloody raincoat."

She shifted onto her back and stretched her arms above her head. "What do you mean? We are not in London, Sebastian. Today you will not need a raincoat. The forecast calls for an abundance of sunshine."

He chuckled. "I meant raincoat as in *condoms*. I've had enough of those annoying rubber ducks to last a lifetime. Sheer torture, I tell you."

The description made her smile. "The reference to a bath toy presents quite a grand visual."

He rolled to his side, bent his elbow for support and propped his jaw on his palm. "What time do we have to be at the wedding?"

"Noon. I have to assist Violet with her dress."

He lowered the sheet, baring Nasira's torso, and laid his cheek beneath her breasts. "I'm certain she has several ladies-in-waiting who will come to her aid."

"Perhaps, but I would like to be a part of the process."

Using a fingertip, he drew circles around her belly. "Then you should definitely get some rest."

"How can I rest with you touching me this way?"

"I am trying to connect with our child."

And that proclamation moved Nasira in unexpected and wonderful ways. "Do you wish for a boy or a girl?"

His hand came to a stop on her belly. "I'm still getting use to the fatherhood idea. I haven't had time to consider the gender."

She stroked his hair. "I personally have no preference, although I could see you with a daughter. She would have you wrapped around her finger in an instant."

"That would mean she's exactly like her mother." He pressed a kiss on her belly then rose up slightly and began to speak softly, sincerely. "Hello there, baby Edwards. This is your old dad. I wanted to introduce myself even though some might believe I've taken total leave of my senses, talking to a tadpole who undoubtedly won't remember this conversation."

He sent Nasira a grin before giving his consideration back to his unborn child. "In the future, beyond your toddler years, you're most likely going to be frustrated with me, and perhaps during your teens, you're going to despise me. At times I might be strict, but you never need to doubt how much I love you, and how much I love this wonderful woman who is currently giving you a safe haven in which to grow. But whatever you decide to become, be it a businessman or a butler, please know I will always be proud of you, and I promise I will always forgive your faults."

Overwhelmed by the sweetness of his words, Nasira battled tears. This time, tears of joy. Of blessed relief. "You will be an amazing father."

He returned to her side and kissed her cheek. "I will be the best father I can be."

"Sebastian, my love, I know in my soul you will be the very best."

Nasira had finally been granted her heart's desire—the gift of a precious baby and the love a good man. She felt as if she were the most fortunate woman in the world. And before she drifted off again, she wished that same good fortune on Rafe and Violet on this day when their life together would truly begin....

"With the power vested in me by the great State of Texas, I now pronounce you husband and wife. Now give that little gal a kiss."

Nothing was more boring than sitting through a wedding, especially when the man presiding over the nuptials was clearly a repressed comedian. Yet Sebastian admittedly enjoyed Nasira squeezing his hand during the vows. And he reluctantly acknowledged that Violet and Rafe's pledge to each other had been rather moving at times.

Bloody hell. He had turned into a lovesick sap. But he wouldn't want it any other way.

After the bride and groom vacated the makeshift altar, Sebastian took his wife by the hand and led her through the hordes of humanity. He had no idea so many people resided in this spot-in-the-road town of Royal.

"I'm going to congratulate Violet and Rafe," Nasira said when they managed to find a small space to stand without bumping into guests. "Are you coming with me?"

Sebastian peered out over the crowd and noticed the lengthy reception line near the white tent. He also spotted one man he needed to speak with out of his wife's earshot. "If you don't mind, I believe I'll find a waiter and get a drink. I'll catch up with you in a bit."

She brushed a kiss across his cheek. "All right, but please hurry. I do not want anyone to assume I put you on a plane to London without me."

He frowned. "Why would anyone assume that?"

"This is a very small town, Sebastian. Gossip travels at the speed of lightning, according to Violet."

Nothing he hadn't encountered in the jolly old town of London. "I'll be along briefly."

After Nasira disappeared in the sea of people, Sebastian set out for Mac McCallum, who was standing near the bar bedecked in white bunting. He could now kill two birds with one stone.

As soon as he reached the drink station, he addressed the bartender, tip in hand. "I need a scotch, neat. The best scotch you have, actually."

The man poured the drink and set it before him. "It's free."

Did he think he was so socially inept that he didn't understand the concept of an open bar? "I realize that," he said as he tossed the fifty-dollar bill on the counter. "This is a tip."

"Thanks a heap, mister."

"You're most welcome, barkeep."

He grabbed the drink, approached Mac and looked around before he began asking questions. Realizing the coast was crystal clear, he addressed the cowboy. "Did you make the arrangements?" he asked in a lowered voice.

"Yeah, I did. Delivered the funds personally."

"What timeline should I expect?"

Mac swiped a hand over his jaw. "You're going completely custom, so I estimate at least a year, maybe a bit longer."

That would allow enough time to finalize the deal before the birth of their child. Odd that only a few weeks ago, he would not allow himself to believe he could continue the Edwards legacy. "I appreciate your help. And by the way, who are all these people?"

Mac leaned back against the bar. "Most are Texas Cattleman's Club members, old and new, and their significant others. The man over there is Ben Rassad, Darin Shakir's cousin. And that guy over there is Gavin McNeal."

"I met the former sheriff at the festival a few weeks ago."

"Yeah, he's part of the old guard. The man standing near him is the new Texas Cattleman's Club president, Case Baxter and his wife, Mellie. I'm surprised he bothered to show up, but I guess he's decided to bury the hatchet. And right over there is the current sheriff, Nathan Battle."

Sebastian sensed a story coming on. "Does this Baxter fellow have a problem with the bride and groom?"

Mac set his empty beer aside and straightened. "It's a long story, but Case was very angry with Rafe for secretly trying to buy up the town, including Mellie's land where the club sits. But all's been settled now that Rafe decided not to get revenge on me for his assumption I defiled your wife a long time ago, and as you probably know, that led to Rafe's torture and confinement by your deceased father-in-law."

The unbelievable story, laid out in such a manner, reeked of a made-for-TV movie plot. And although he now knew the details, and that Mac had no designs on Nasira, he still wasn't pleased with the man using *defiled* and *his wife* in the same sentence. "Regardless, I'm glad the situation has been resolved."

He was also glad to see his spouse weaving through the masses, heading his way. When she arrived, he slipped his arm around her slender waist. "Did you give the happy couple my regards?"

"Unfortunately I could not reach them. Fortunately we have time to visit with them before our flight departs tonight." She turned her smile on Mac. "I spoke with Andrea a few moments ago. I believe she is searching for you."

The man's expression lit up like a livewire. "She's probably wondering about the documents I left her yesterday. You folks enjoy the rest of the day, and have a safe flight."

Nasira laughed as soon as Mac left the immediate premises. "Did you notice how quickly he left when I mentioned his assistant's name?"

"I did. Obviously she is very efficient."

She frowned. "She is very attractive, and Mac is completely smitten. I would not be surprised to learn they are the next couple to wed in Royal."

Honestly, Sebastian didn't care about anyone other than the woman standing next to him, looking stunning in her coral chiffon gown and matching heels. He crooked his finger in invitation. "I would greatly appreciate some alone time with my wife."

She took a moment to survey the frantic scene. "That could be difficult to come by unless I borrow a cattle prod to clear the crowd."

Cattle prod? Obviously his wife had resided in Texas long enough to adopt the classic cowboy colloquialisms. "I don't see anyone milling about that massive statue of the woman Gavin McNeal mentioned at the fair."

Nasira peered off into the distance. "Oh, yes, the statue of Jess Golden, his wife's distant relative. If we hurry, perhaps we might steal some privacy, although we will have ample alone time on the plane."

He liked the sound of that, yet he refused to wait until they boarded the jet to let her in on his secret plan. He felt like an impetuous schoolboy on Christmas Eve as he guided her toward the legendary figure from Texas Cattleman's Club's past. Once they arrived, he gave his beautiful bride a kiss and as an added bonus, a pat on her shapely bottom.

"I spoke with Mac earlier today," he began, "and he told me that at one time, the Texas Cattleman's Club members engaged in missions bordering on espionage. Apparently it was quite the rage back then."

She favored him with an endearing smile. "You cannot believe everything you hear, although I admit, I have heard the same. However, clearly times have changed."

He looked lovingly at Nasira and in that moment recognized the value of family and love. "I'd personally like to believe that men of honor still have the capacity to come to the rescue of their fair maidens."

She touched his face with reverence. "They do. After all, you have rescued me from a life without a child, fathered by the man I love with all my heart and soul."

"You have done the same for me. I want nothing more than to have you as the mother of our children, my love. And to reward you for your efforts, I have a gift to present you."

Her sunny expression melted into a frown. "You have already given me the best gift I could have ever wished for. Our baby-to-be."

She had given him more than he could express. "This will be something we can all enjoy as a family."

"Is it bigger than a music box?"

"Much bigger."

"Where is it?"

"It is being built as of tomorrow."

She looked entirely confused. "Sebastian, I have the Bentley. I do not need another car."

"It's not a car, sweetheart. It's a house."

She appeared unimpressed. "We already own two houses."

"And we shall have three, only this one is a vacation home and will not be located in the UK."

"Tahiti?"

"No. Royal."

Worried that he might have permanently rendered her speechless, he waited for her shock to subside. "Why? Where?"

"In the gated golf community of Pine Valley. I selected a lot and I met with the architect after you left me to return to Rafe's. It's a place we can call home when we return next year on holiday."

Her eyes brightened. "Oh, Sebastian, that would be marvelous. By that time, we will have our baby and we can introduce him or her to its new cousin."

Knowing he had pleased her pleased Sebastian greatly. "I vow to make this home as extravagant as you like."

She wrapped her arms around his neck and held him tightly for a time. "My dear sweet love, my home is anywhere you are."

This incredible woman, his wife, the mother of his child, had changed him in ways he had never believed possible. "And I promise you this day, beneath this historic statue and this symbol of bygone days, I will be there for you and our children through good times and bad."

She pulled away and stared at him. "Children?"

"Certainly. At least five. However, you do realize that will require quite a bit of practice, beginning tonight in the sleeping quarters on the plane."

"I am already pregnant, Sebastian."

"My dear, practice does make perfect."

As they rejoined the celebrants and sought out the bride and groom, Sebastian Edwards realized that perfection was in his reach. He had a remarkable wife, the promise of a bright future and a love he had resisted out of fear. He had learned to forgive when forgiveness had not come easily for him, yet he had his lovely bride to thank for that. The moment he returned home, he would seek out his father and afford him the benevolence Nasira had taught him, before it was too late to mend their relationship.

Ten years ago, the confirmed bachelor and billionaire had entered into a convenient marriage with an exotic stranger. He had done so to produce the requisite heir but had abandoned that plan and refused to entertain the idea of having children when she'd miscarried. For her part, Nasira had married to escape a life dictated by her father's belief she wasn't worthy to choose her own mate. Never in a million years would Sebastian have believed this arrangement would result in undeniable, unconditional love.

Life was good, and he predicted it would only grow better with each passing day. Forgiveness was his for the taking, and love would forever be the constant that ruled his life. Not business. Not gold. Only Nasira.

Always Nasira.

* * * * *

Don't miss a single installment of
TEXAS CATTLEMAN'S CLUB:
LIES AND LULLABIES
Baby Secrets and a Scheming Sheikh Rock
Royal, Texas

* * *

If you're on Twitter, tell us what you think
of Harlequin Desire! #harlequindesire

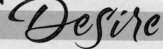
Available June 7, 2016

#2449 REDEEMING THE BILLIONAIRE SEAL
Billionaires and Babies • by Lauren Canan
Navy SEAL Chance Masters is only back on the family ranch until his next deployment, but can the all-grown-up girl next door struggling to raise her infant niece convince him his rightful place is at home?

#2450 A BRIDE FOR THE BOSS
Texas Cattleman's Club: Lies and Lullabies
by Maureen Child
When Mac's overworked assistant quits, he's left floundering. But when she challenges the wealthy rancher to spend two weeks not working—with *her*—he soon realizes all the pleasures he's been missing...

#2451 A PREGNANCY SCANDAL
Love and Lipstick • by Kat Cantrell
One broken rule. One night of passion. Now...one accidental pregnancy! A marriage of convenience is the only way to prevent a scandal for the popular senator and his no-frills CFO lover—until their union becomes so much more...

#2452 THE BOSS AND HIS COWGIRL
Red Dirt Royalty • by Silver James
Clay Barron is an oil magnate bred for great things. Nothing can stop his ambition—except the beautiful assistant from his hometown. Will his craving for the former cowgirl mean a choice between love and success?

#2453 ARRANGED MARRIAGE, BEDROOM SECRETS
Courtesan Brides • by Yvonne Lindsay
To prepare for his arranged marriage, Prince Thierry hires a mysterious beauty to tutor him in romance. His betrothed, Mila, mischievously takes the woman's place. But as the prince falls for his "forbidden" lover, Mila's revelations will threaten all they hold dear...

#2454 TRAPPED WITH THE MAVERICK MILLIONAIRE
From Mavericks to Married • by Joss Wood
Years ago, one kiss from a hockey superstar rocked Rory's world. Now Mac needs her—as his live-in physical therapist! Despite their explosive chemistry, she keeps her hands off—until one hot island night as a storm rages...

YOU CAN FIND MORE INFORMATION ON UPCOMING HARLEQUIN® TITLES, FREE EXCERPTS AND MORE AT WWW.HARLEQUIN.COM.

HDCNM0516

REQUEST YOUR FREE BOOKS!

2 FREE NOVELS PLUS 2 FREE GIFTS!

⬦ HARLEQUIN®

Desire

ALWAYS POWERFUL, PASSIONATE AND PROVOCATIVE

YES! Please send me 2 FREE Harlequin® Desire novels and my 2 FREE gifts (gifts are worth about $10). After receiving them, if I don't wish to receive any more books, I can return the shipping statement marked "cancel." If I don't cancel, I will receive 6 brand-new novels every month and be billed just $4.55 per book in the U.S. or $5.24 per book in Canada. That's a savings of at least 13% off the cover price! It's quite a bargain! Shipping and handling is just 50¢ per book in the U.S. and 75¢ per book in Canada.* I understand that accepting the 2 free books and gifts places me under no obligation to buy anything. I can always return a shipment and cancel at any time. Even if I never buy another book, the two free books and gifts are mine to keep forever.

225/326 HDN GH2P

Name	(PLEASE PRINT)	
Address		Apt. #
City	State/Prov.	Zip/Postal Code

Signature (if under 18, a parent or guardian must sign)

Mail to the **Reader Service:**

IN U.S.A.: P.O. Box 1867, Buffalo, NY 14240-1867
IN CANADA: P.O. Box 609, Fort Erie, Ontario L2A 5X3

Want to try two free books from another line?
Call 1-800-873-8635 or visit www.ReaderService.com.

* Terms and prices subject to change without notice. Prices do not include applicable taxes. Sales tax applicable in N.Y. Canadian residents will be charged applicable taxes. Offer not valid in Quebec. This offer is limited to one order per household. Not valid for current subscribers to Harlequin Desire books. All orders subject to credit approval. Credit or debit balances in a customer's account(s) may be offset by any other outstanding balance owed by or to the customer. Please allow 4 to 6 weeks for delivery. Offer available while quantities last.

Your Privacy—The Reader Service is committed to protecting your privacy. Our Privacy Policy is available online at www.ReaderService.com or upon request from the Reader Service.

We make a portion of our mailing list available to reputable third parties that offer products we believe may interest you. If you prefer that we not exchange your name with third parties, or if you wish to clarify or modify your communication preferences, please visit us at www.ReaderService.com/consumerschoice or write to us at Reader Service Preference Service, P.O. Box 9062, Buffalo, NY 14240-9062. Include your complete name and address.

HDI5

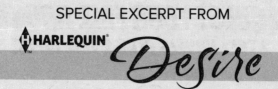
It had been a long day, but a good one.

Andi was feeling pretty smug about her decision to
quit her job and deliberately ignoring the occasional
twinges of regret. She should have done it three years
ago. As soon as she realized she was in love with a man
who would never see her as more than a piece of office
equipment.

Her heart ached a little, but she took another sip of
wine and purposefully drowned that pain. Once she was
free of her idle daydreams of Mac, she'd be able to look
around, find a man to be with. To help her build the life
she wanted so badly.

Her arms ached from wielding a paint roller, but
working on her home felt good. So good, in fact, she didn't
even grumble when someone knocked on the front door.

Wineglass in hand, she answered the door and jolted when Mac smiled at her.

"Mac? What're you doing here?"

"Hello to you, too," he said and stepped past her, unasked, into the house.

All she could do was close the door and follow him into the living room.

He turned around and gave her a quick smile that had her stomach jittering in response before she could quash her automatic response. "The color's good."

"Thanks. Mac, why are you here?"

"I'm here because I wanted to get a look at what you left me for." His gaze fixed on her and for the first time, he noticed that she wore a tiny tank top and a silky pair of drawstring pants. Her feet were bare and her toenails were painted a soft blush pink. Her hair was long and loose over her shoulders, just skimming the tops of her breasts.

Mac took a breath and wondered where that flash of heat had come from. He'd been with Andi nearly every day for the past six years and he'd never reacted to her like this before.

Now it seemed to be all he could notice.

Whatever You're Into... Passionate Reads

Looking for more passionate reads from Harlequin®?
Fear not! Harlequin® Presents, Harlequin® Desire and
Harlequin® Blaze offer you irresistible romance stories
featuring powerful heroes.

♦HARLEQUIN *Presents*®

Do you want alpha males, decadent glamour and jet-set
lifestyles? Step into the sensational, sophisticated world of
Harlequin® Presents, where sinfully tempting heroes ignite a
fierce and wickedly irresistible passion!

♦HARLEQUIN® *Desire*

Harlequin® Desire novels are powerful, passionate and
provocative contemporary romances set against a backdrop of
wealth, privilege and sweeping family saga. Alpha heroes with
a soft side meet strong-willed but vulnerable heroines amid a
dramatic world of divided loyalties, high-stakes conflict and
intense emotion.

♦HARLEQUIN® *Blaze*®

Harlequin® Blaze stories sizzle with strong heroines and
irresistible heroes playing the game of modern love and lust.
They're fun, sexy and always steamy.

Be sure to check out our full selection of books
within each series every month!

www.Harlequin.com

HPASSION2016

HARLEQUIN®

A Romance FOR EVERY MOOD™

Love the Harlequin book you just read?

Your opinion matters.

Review this book on your favorite book site, review site, blog or your own social media properties and share your opinion with other readers!